The Awakening

~ Entangled ~
Christina & Michael
© 2016 Jill Sanders

Follow Jill online at:
Jill@JillSanders.com
Web: http://JillSanders.com
Twitter: @JillMSanders
Facebook: JillSandersBooks
Sign up for Jill's Newsletter @ JillSanders.com

Jill Sanders

Summary

Christina swore she'd never return to her hometown of Hidden Creek, Georgia again. Her upbringing there could only be described as torture at best. She never asked for the unusual abilities she possesses, but was quite certain they would torment her the rest of her life. After spending years hiding and trying to escape the judgement and abuse of her family and the cruel people of Hidden Creek, she's finally come to terms with her gift. But with her parent's sudden passing, it now falls on Christina to return and take care of everything. With her parents gone, she finally hopes to close this dark chapter of her life and leave Hidden Creek behind for good. That is, until she finds herself mysteriously drawn to the intoxicating gentleman next-door, who seems to share a strange and unusual bond with her.

Michael has spent years in the military and on the police force in Atlanta. After almost losing his life in a brutal betrayal by his crooked partner, he's decided to leave the force and take up residence in sleepy, stress-free Hidden Creek, where he meets Christina, a mysterious, raven-haired beauty with uncanny abilities. He'd always thought of himself as a rational person. He didn't buy into in crazy things like; ghosts, spirits, demons, or other paranormal witchcraft nonsense. But now he must be losing it, as a strange apparition begins appearing at the foot of his bed each night.

Jill Sanders

4

The Awakening

by
Jill Sanders

Jill Sanders

Chapter One

Xtina hated the short drive from the small town of Hidden Creek to the older home on the hill where she'd grown up. It was a drive she'd taken many times in her twenty-five years, but one that still haunted her. The roads were slick from the new rainfall and since it was outside of the town limits, there were no streetlights to guide the way.

She passed by a dozen homes, all spaced out with multiple acres in between. Neighbors that weren't really neighbors, just people whose land bordered each other's. She'd known all too well that keeping people at bay had been a priority for her parents. Her heart sank at the thought of attending their funeral tomorrow afternoon, even as other darker thoughts about them crept into her mind.

When she approached the sharp bend in the road where her father had apparently lost control of his truck a few days ago, she slowed. She saw the large gash in the trees and felt a shiver run up her spine. It was a normal reaction to seeing a place where people had died unexpectedly. It was something most people overlooked, but Xtina knew better.

Punching the gas pedal, she continued on the road until she finally turned into the long dirt lane that led to the two-story historical mansion her family had called home since the bricks had been laid by slaves in the early 1800s. It was too dark to see the house from here, but she stopped at the entrance anyway. Even in the darkness, she could feel the eeriness of the place. Moss hung in long strings like spider webs from the thick branches of the tall oaks that lined the driveway. Memories flooded back in her mind and caused her to shiver once more.

Her body ached in places where her father's belt had connected or where her mother's hand had slapped at her. Her heart hurt at the emotional scars they'd inflicted. All the names, all the horrible things they'd said about her, to her. Even as a child, she'd known what they were saying was wrong. She wasn't a devil child.

Shaking off the bad mood, she rolled her hybrid car slowly down the drive. When the house finally did come into view of her headlights, she braced for another onslaught of shivers, but this time, none came.

"Interesting," she murmured to herself as she continued all the way to the end of the bumpy lane and parked behind her mother's old sedan. Turning off her car, she sat in the darkness and listened to the silence, letting her feelings wash over her.

Nothing. Absolutely nothing. She didn't feel… anything. None of the hurt or fear or anger she'd expected.

It was probably due to her weariness from the day's travel. It had been a long drive from the mountains of Colorado to the Southeast. She'd taken her time getting there. After all, what could she do that her grandmother hadn't already taken care of?

Sighing, she thought about her grandmother. The woman was approaching eighty. She was the only one in her family to ever show her kindness, though she had turned a deaf ear to her pleas to move in with her. Her grandmother had probably assumed that Christina was just a normal adolescent child who hated her parents. She wished her grandmother would have listened to her more closely.

Getting out of the car, she opened the back door and pulled out one of her many bags. She'd learned to travel light a few years back, so she could fit everything she owned into four large bags and a small overnight bag.

She only needed the one bag for the night so she left the other bags to bring inside in the daylight tomorrow. After all, it wasn't as if she was going anywhere anytime soon.

She held her breath as she took the first step onto the wide wood porch, waiting for the feelings and emotions to flood in. Once more, nothing happened. Taking another step, she reached the top stair and turned to look down towards the swing. She'd spent countless hours as a child hiding out on that very spot. Hoping, dreaming, talking to whoever would listen to her plight.

Now, the old swing hung in the darkness of the porch, empty of everything she'd once held dear.

Reaching into her pocket, she grabbed her keyring and flipped to the old house key she'd never had the heart to remove. The silver key slid into the lock like a hot knife in butter.

When the door opened, a wave of scented air hit her, causing memories to surface, forcing her to take a step back and drop her bag at her feet. Here were the old feelings she'd been expecting. Holding her breath, she rushed into the room, keeping the front door open wide as she raced across the room to the large windows along the front. She opened every one, along with the back door. By the time she finally settled down, the house was as cold as it was outside.

Finally, she felt like she could breathe freely. She picked up the bag she'd dropped outside and turned to head back inside, but she paused when she saw a light coming from the old McCullen place. No one had lived in the home next door since Christina was six. She remembered the night the last person had moved out of the small place ike it was yesterday.

Another shiver ran down her spine. This time she didn't ignore it. Setting her bag inside the door, she tucked her keys deep in her pocket and started across the side yard. The place was smaller than her family's place. Her family had owned one of the largest plantations south of Atlanta, so all of the neighboring homes paled next to theirs.

The McCullen place was the nearest neighbor, a modest three-bedroom ranch home. Seeing a light come from the window was cause to investigate. The house had sat empty her entire childhood for a good reason.

***

It wasn't a noise that woke Michael from his deep sleep. It was the lack of noises that had his eyes sliding open in the middle of the night. The same lack of noise that had woken him every single night for almost an entire year.

When he'd first chosen to relocate to the small town of Hidden Creek, he'd thought he'd found his little slice of paradise. The town seemed to be just what he needed. Small, quaint, and—a big bonus—it had a low crime rate. The old ranch house he'd snatched up in an auction had been reasonably priced and, with a few repairs, exactly what he needed. Something to keep his mind off the dreadful night that had caused him so much pain, both physically and mentally.

Instead, what he'd gained was a different kind of nightmare, one that he could find no explanation for.

Since he was still seeing a shrink from his time on the Atlanta force, he'd opened up to the woman about what he was experiencing, only to be ridiculed and told he was having some sort of PTSD moment. After she'd written him a stack of new prescriptions and upped their visits to twice a week, he'd decided to start keeping things to himself.

After a few months of hitting a brick wall, he stopped seeing the psychiatrist and started his own deeper research into his unique problem. He'd come up with nothing more than crackpots and hearsay accounts. Nothing solid.

He'd spent years on the force as a detective, three as lead after their last head of the department retired. He knew how to dig deep to find answers, but when it came to ghost hunting, he was stumped.

Switching on the light, he blinked a few times, letting his eyes adjust to the brightness. He knew what was going to happen next.

Even though every window in his house was sealed tight when he'd gone to bed, a blast of cold air hit him full force, almost taking his breath away.

There she stood, at the foot of his bed. Her long frail arms were stretched out towards him, as if asking him for help. The yellow gown was draped over her thin body, as if she'd hastily pulled it on. It flew around her as if floating in water, as did her hair. One side of the gown had fallen, exposing the creamy whiteness of her shoulder. The woman was young and beautiful, if you didn't look into her eyes and see the complete look of horror on her face.

He tried each night to notice more about her, but all he could see was the emptiness of those dark spots where her eyes should have been and the silent plea of her outstretched arms. He could never see far enough down to notice how long the gown was or if she was wearing shoes, but something inside him told him that she wasn't.

As the wind whirled around him, his eyes locked with hers. Her mouth opened in a silent scream, which always caused the air to almost freeze over his skin.

He'd tried many times to snap a picture or a video of her, but each time, the electronics would freeze up or just stop working until after she was gone. He'd even spent a few hundred dollars on an old camera, one without microchips or batteries. Still, nothing had shown up. Only darkness.

He watched in silent horror as she took a step closer to him, knowing she was moments away from dissipating. This time, he was shocked to see her head jerk to the left, towards the bedroom window.

She'd never done that before. She took a step towards the window, and the darkness in her eyes retreated until only sadness remained. Her arms reached towards the window as the sheer curtains billowed softly. Michael's eyes traveled to the spot where her eyes were locked, and his heart kicked when he noticed a pale face staring back in. A beautiful face. The woman's green eyes weren't on him, but zeroed in on the figure standing at the end of his bed.

Instead of shock on the newcomer's face, there was a slight smile on her lips, as if she was seeing an old friend. His first thought was that now there were two ghosts haunting him, one inside his house and the other outside.

But then the woman's green eyes moved towards his own and finally fear registered on her face. At the moment when their eyes connected, the ghostly figure disappeared from the foot of his bed and the wind instantly died down.

Slowly, everything returned to normal. The sounds of the crickets, the soft breeze of the air, the smell of the night's fresh rain. His eyes moved back to the window. The green-eyed woman was still standing outside, looking at him. When he moved to get up, she gasped and quickly turned around.

He'd spent the last year in fear and ready for just about anything, so his mind snapped to attention and it took him no time to slip on a pair of pants and wiggle into some shoes. He was out his front door in less than a minute. He caught up with the woman before she got too far.

Yanking on her shoulders, he pulled her to a stop at the edge of his property.

"Who the hell are you?" he demanded as his fingers sank into flesh. She was real. Flesh and bone. He could smell her perfume mixed with the scent of wildflowers that he'd planted along the fence line.

"I… I'm sorry. I didn't know someone was living here." She tried to take a step back, her hands coming up to circle his wrists. Her sexy lips went from a pout to a frown as her eyes locked on his hand touching her.

"Who are you?" he asked again, this time a little more softly.

"I'm… I'm Xtina…" She shook her head quickly, sending her dark hair flying as her eyes moved up his arm slowly. "Christina Warren. I live next door." She jerked her head towards the house a few yards away.

"Oh." He dropped his arm when he remembered that the older couple who lived there had just died in a car accident a few days back. "I'm sorry about…"

"My parents," she said dryly, giving him the hint that she wasn't all that moved by what had happened. It didn't take years on the force to read that in her eyes.

15

"Sorry about your parents. If you need anything..." He dropped off when he noticed that her eyes were glued on his house. She didn't look like she was about to break down or start crying over her parents. They remained silent for a moment, then he jumped in. "You saw her." It was more a statement than a question.

Her green eyes moved up to his and he watched as they clouded over. "Who?"

"The ghost." He felt like an idiot the second those words left his lips. When he noticed that her green eyes softened, he held his breath. At least she hadn't laughed at him. After a moment of silence, he finally said, "I saw you look directly at her."

He waited, then she released a soft breath and she nodded. "She's not a ghost." He almost laughed, but the determined look in her eyes stopped him. Her shoulders slumped. "I've seen her my entire life."

"Who is—?" he started to ask, but then paused. "Your entire life?" When she nodded, he swallowed. "Do you know who she is?"

She shook her head slightly. "No, my parents never would tell me anything about who lived there before Mr. and Mrs. McCullen."

"What happened to the McCullens?" he asked, watching her eyes dart back to his home. A million more questions raged through his mind, but he doubted she'd give him the opportunity to ask them all as they stood in the dirt.

"They retired to Mexico before I was born." She glanced back over at him and even in the darkness, he could tell she wasn't telling him something.

"What...?" He started to take a step towards her, but her shoulders stiffened and her gaze darted towards her home.

"I didn't get your name." Her entire body stiffened.

"Oh, right, sorry. I'm Michael Kincaid. Mike," he corrected as he reached out his hand for hers. When she just frowned down at his hand, he shoved it into his jean pocket. "I bought the place from the bank about a year ago."

She dipped her head in acknowledgement. "Welcome to the neighborhood." When she took a step back, he felt a shiver up his spine. Almost like his ghost was watching them from the window of his room. Glancing over his shoulder, he saw only darkness in his window. "Maybe..." He turned back to her. "Okay, this might sound weird, and you have every right to say no." He held his breath until she finally jumped in.

"Go ahead." She kept her eyes on his.

"Well, it's just that now that I'm up, I mean, every time she wakes me, I can't get back to sleep."

She slowly crossed her arms over her chest and

her green eyes darkened.

"Maybe you'd like to come over for a cup of tea?" he blurted out.

She didn't laugh at him, and he added it to the list of things he immediately liked about her. She did, however, bite her bottom lip. His eyes were glued to the motion and an instant flash of desire spiked, something he hadn't felt in a very long time. She was very beautiful. Her rich dark hair fell long down her back; she wore short spiky bangs that accented her green eyes. It was a little too dark to see if she wore makeup, but something told him that she didn't wear as much as his last girlfriend had.

She was tall, almost as tall as he was and her legs looked damn sexy in the tight black leggings she was wearing. The short boots added height to her and made those long legs look even more appealing.

"How about you help me bring in all my stuff and I see what my folks left in their cupboards instead?"

"Really?" He couldn't hide the relief from his voice, causing her to chuckle softly.

"Really. This way, if you get out of hand, I can use my great-grandfather's shotgun on you." She winked and turned back towards her car.

"Thanks." He fell into step with her, not wanting to turn back towards his house.

"Why don't you sell the place?" she asked when she opened the trunk of her car.

"I just bought it," he retorted. "Besides, I'm not done fixing it up yet. There's still a lot that needs to be done." He reached in and took out two bags and hoisted them over his shoulders. "To the place. I mean, I have no carpet, I need to lay the flooring…"

"Okay, I get it." She picked up the last small bag. "So you plan on selling it once you're done?" she asked as they made their way up the stairs towards the front door. He noticed that all the windows to the house were wide open, including the front door.

"Haven't figured that out yet. Airing the place out?" He frowned at the chill in the air when he stepped in.

"You could say that." She dumped her bag just inside the door next to another one, then walked over and cranked up the thermostat.

He felt a shiver up his spine and wished he'd thought to grab a jacket. It wasn't quite warm enough anymore to go running around in the middle of the night without one. Soon the days and nights would be cool enough that he'd never leave the house without one.

"We can start a fire. The old stove usually heats up the house quickly." She nodded towards the cast iron that sat in the corner of the room. He set her bags down next to the other two and walked over to build a fire as she went around shutting the windows.

"I'll go see what's in the kitchen. I'm sure there's still enough food in there to feed an army." He watched her disappear into the back hallway. As he finished building the fire, he heard her banging pots and pans in the next room and decided to take a look around the big room.

He'd admired the huge place for over a year. Her parents had been private people, too private to ever invite him inside. The large winding staircase was something to look at. He imagined it had been a bitch to build. He looked around and guessed that must have been in the early 1800s. He didn't know the history of the place, but after living in the small town for about a year, he knew that it had always belonged to the Warren family.

He guessed that this place was way older than his house, and in a million times better shape. Here, the furniture was dated, but still had years of life left. He frowned when he realized that the large room didn't have a television in it. He'd never seen a home without at least a forty-inch flat screen before.

His eye caught on a wall next to the stairs filled with family photos. He walked over and glanced quickly at them, then noticed that the majority were in black and white and had been taken before the turn of the century.

There was only one photo of Christina and he guessed she'd been around five years old. Her long hair was a stark blonde and was pulled back tight in long braids. Her green eyes looked lost and she looked like she was on the verge of tears. He supposed it was a school photo, but he couldn't be sure.

He heard her curse just as a crash sounded from the kitchen. When he walked in, she was on the floor picking up the shattered pieces of a mug.

"I always hated this stupid…" She broke off as her voice hitched.

He felt like running back to his house, but something held him there. It was the lost look in her eyes that dug deep into his heart. Instead of leaving, he walked over and gathered her into his arms and held her as she cried.

Jill Sanders

Chapter Two

 $\mathcal{S}$ tupid. She was being stupid. She'd thought that she'd cried all her tears years ago, but seeing her mother's favorite mug had caused her hands to shake. Then she'd dropped the damn thing and the only feeling that flooded her was relief that it was gone. That they were gone.

So, she'd cried for her freedom and for her lost childhood. When she finally came back to her senses, she realized just how wonderful it felt to be held. Then she froze in place as her breath hitched. She waited, ready to jerk away at any moment, but nothing happened. Nothing.

She didn't get the expected zing up her back, or the fire shooting through her veins. Testing herself, she reached out and touched his bare arm and held her breath. When all she felt was his warm skin under her palm, she leaned back.

"I'm sorry." She looked into his brown eyes, expecting… something. But, once more, nothing happened except his lips curving upward in a slight smile.

"I'd say you were due a good cry. After losing your folks." He dropped his arms and stood up, then held out his hand for hers. She'd avoided shaking his hand the first time, but she was curious and took it this time.

Once more, all she felt was the warmth of his palm, the scratch of his calloused hand against her softer, smaller one.

"Is something wrong?" He glanced down at their joined hands, breaking her from her spell.

"No." She quickly pulled herself up with his help. "I guess the long drive is finally getting to me."

He nodded, then glanced over when her mother's old-fashioned kettle started whistling.

"Wow, I haven't seen one of those since…" He chuckled. "Ever, actually. At least not in person."

She walked over and removed it from the flame. "My folks were a little… old school." She glanced over her shoulder. "I hope you're okay with oolong."

"I might be if I knew what it was," he joked.

She smiled. "It's a kind of calming tea. My mother swore by it. I prefer green tea myself, but since she never would…" She dropped off when she realized he probably didn't want to hear her life story. "Anyway, it's okay with a couple scoops of honey or sugar."

He nodded, then walked over and leaned against the counter.

"Do you have any brothers or sisters?" he asked.

"No, I'm an only child." She felt another wave cross over her core and turned to the task of preparing the tea.

"I have a brother," he said, glancing around.

"It must have been nice growing up," she said, dumping some honey into her cup, then she walked over to the large walk-in pantry and pulled out a box of crackers.

"It had its perks. Our folks could never really tell who had caused most of the trouble." He chuckled. "So, naturally we either got out of punishment, or we both got punished, depending on the extent of the damage."

She smiled and leaned into the fridge to pull out some of the smoked cheese her father always loved.

"Can I help?" His voice came from right behind her, causing her to jump slightly.

"No," she said, straightening up. "I've got this. If you want, you can carry the tea in while I put this on a platter."

"Sure." He took the two mugs and walked into the living room. She could already feel the warmth from the fire radiating into the house.

Setting the plate of cheese and crackers on the coffee table, she took her mug from his hands and sat down in her mother's leather recliner. "Please." She motioned for him to sit next to her in her father's matching chair.

"You're right, it warmed up quickly in here. Looks like I'll need to make plans to install one of these." He motioned towards the iron stove.

"You only need a fire once in a while around here, but when you do, it's nice to have one. How long have you been seeing her?" she asked after taking a sip of her tea. Even with a large dollop of honey and two teaspoons of sugar, she still cringed at the memories the tea brought up.

"I moved in about a year ago, so…" He tilted his head and thought about it. "Since that first night." He shivered, a standard sign of the first fleeting hints of the supernatural.

"What has she said or done?"

"Said?" he asked and his face lost all of its color. Reaching over, she touched his hand.

"It's okay, I doubt she can actually talk." She held in a chuckle and watched his color return.

"Um, all she does is stand there, with her arms out towards me. Freaking me out every night."

"What do you feel when she's around?" She

26

popped a cracker with cheese into her mouth. She hadn't stopped for dinner, since she'd wanted to be home before sun-up. Now, her stomach was rewarding her with large growls and pains.

"Loneliness," he answered, taking another sip of his tea.

"Yes." She sighed and ate another cracker.

"Why are you so sure she's not a ghost?" He leaned closer as he put his elbows on his knees, his brown eyes getting more intense.

She wasn't sure how to explain the differences. Instead, she chose to ask him more questions.

"Why are you so sure she is one?"

He chuckled and leaned back in his chair. "Now you're sounding like my shrink. Always turning my questions around and asking me other ones."

Her eyebrows drew up. "You're seeing a psychiatrist?"

He smiled. "A grown man tells you he's seeing what he believes is a ghost for the last year… so, yeah, I'm seeing a psychiatrist."

She sighed and rested back.

"I'm not crazy," he broke in. "At least…"

She opened her eyes and could see the worry cross his eyes. Eyes that somehow looked familiar. Then it dawned on her. She'd seen the same look everyday of her life staring back at her in the mirror.

"No, you're not crazy." She wanted to reach across and touch his hand but held back.

"Has anyone else lived in the place since the McCullens?" he asked after a moment of silence, steering them off the dark path their conversation had turned down.

She took her time answering, then slowly nodded. "Yes, just one other person."

"Did he or she ever see the woman?" He leaned forward again, and she could tell he was trying to solve the same puzzle she'd tried to solve once before.

"No." Xtina felt the shiver run down her spine. This one had nothing to do with the supernatural. "He only lived there for a summer." She picked up her mug and finished the tea in one swallow, trying to clear the sour thoughts from her mind.

"Well, then." Mike leaned back in the chair and rested his head back. "I guess the question is, why us?"

She looked at him, her eyebrows going up. He leaned forward and set his almost-empty mug down next to the plate of crackers. "I know for a fact that others can't see her."

"Oh?" She set her mug down and picked up another cracker, nibbling on it slowly so he couldn't see her fingers shake.

"Yes, my brother, Ethan, spent the night once.

When I woke him, he laughed at me. She was standing there just like tonight, only…"

"He couldn't see her," she supplied.

"Yeah, why do you suppose that is? That he couldn't see her?"

"Maybe she didn't want him to see her."

"What the hell does that mean?" His voice sounded tired. "Why me? Why you?" He ran his hands through his hair, ruffling it and making it stick up. Somehow, it only caused him to look even sexier than before.

She shrugged. "Does she scare you?"

"Doesn't she scare you?" he almost chocked out.

"No." She shook her head lightly. "Never."

He was silent for a moment. "You sit over there, telling me that seeing a ghost…" When he noticed her eyebrows shoot up, he cleared his throat. "Or whatever she is, that it doesn't scare you. You're the kind of person who invites a stranger into your house at…"—he glanced down at his watch and whistled— "three in the morning. I could be a psycho, a murderer or a…" He shook off that thought then turned to her. "What exactly does scare you?"

She looked at him for a moment, then decided to tell him the truth.

"My parents," she said under her breath as she

felt a zip down her entire body.

***

Mike couldn't help being shocked. He knew she was seeing it in his eyes and on his face, so he leaned down and took up his mug again and drank the rest of the honeyed liquid.

"They must have done something right."

"Not really." Then she laughed. "Actually, they died. I guess you can say that was something in my favor."

He glanced towards the door, wondering if he should be the one worrying about his own well-being.

Then she laughed. "Now you're thinking I'm the crazy one." When he just continued to look at her, she finished. "I'm sorry, I guess you'd have to know how I was raised to understand." She leaned back and rested her head back, much like he'd just done. "Don't worry, I'm not a murderer or a…" She smiled over at him. "I'm just a bitter daughter who was stripped of her childhood because my parents thought I was evil for seeing things, for feeling things, for… being different."

He frowned and leaned towards her. "But, she's real." It was more a question than a statement.

"Yes," she agreed, "she's real. So are other things."

"Okay, now you're officially freaking me out." He stood up and walked over to the fire, hoping

30

that the sudden chill he'd gotten was from his nerves instead of… He quickly glanced around the room.

"No, the place is clean. I've only seen her near your house. As for the rest…" He watched as a shiver racked her body. "It has always come and gone without notice."

"Some childhood."

"Yes." Her voice was low and he could tell she had grown tired.

"Okay, you and I have to finish this some other time." He walked over and set his mug down next to hers. "I can tell you need rest and I have a few hours before I have to get to work."

"Work?" She stood up and followed him towards the door.

"Well, my work." He chuckled at the private joke. "If you can call it that. I spend half my days working on the house and the other on the computer."

"You work from home?"

He nodded and smiled. "Another time then? Maybe you can come over tomorrow for dinner."

"Can't." He watched sadness creep into her green eyes. "The funeral is tomorrow followed by a dinner here." She looked up at him. "If you feel like it, you're welcome to stop by. There will be plenty of food."

"Of course. I didn't really know your parents all that much, but your father was nice to me when I saw him. What time and can I bring anything?"

She smiled. "It starts at six and you could bring a bottle of wine, since I know there isn't any here and none of my parents' friends would dare partake. Nor would they condone the drink in my parents' home."

He smiled. "Then I'll bring a couple bottles and we can have some drinks after everyone leaves."

"I think we're going to get along just great," she said, leaning on the open door. "Good night, Michael."

"Good night, Xtina," he said, making sure to use the name he guessed made her more comfortable. Then he reached out, not sure why he did, and ran a finger down the side of her cheek. When he headed back across the yard towards his place, he felt her watch him as he crossed the yard. Warmth spread through him knowing she was so focused on him. He couldn't explain the instant draw he'd had towards her, other than the fact that she was another human being that had witnessed something that no one else could.

When he stepped into his house, the air seemed warmer, friendlier somehow.

Walking back to his room, he paused just outside the door and peeked in. The room was empty. Letting out the breath he'd been holding, he decided to start work early and headed into his office. He had a few clients whose files he needed to update after working on them this last week. He loved his new job, something he hadn't been able to say for a long time.

Since the accident over a year ago, he'd been debating what to do. He'd received a nice settlement check for his pain and trouble. Big enough to put a chunk down on the house and start the remodeling process. The monthly settlement checks helped keep him eating until he'd started Kincaid Investigations.

He had quickly gained clients through word of mouth from some of his buddies still on the force. Over the first several months, the number of clients had grown and he was slowly becoming so busy, he was actually thinking of hiring some help, someone who could handle the mundane office chores he so detested. He hoped he'd get big enough to add another investigator in a year or so.

Digging into people's backgrounds for a living had turned him cautious. He supposed that's why he'd been so abrasive with Christina at first. Trust was something he was working on, but after what he'd been through, who could blame him?

He knew it was bad, but his fingers itched to type her name into the computer and find out more about the sexy, dark-haired beauty next door. Instead, he opened up the local paper and reread about her parents' accident.

Over an hour later, he flipped his computer off

and frowned as he made his way into the bedroom to pull on his jogging clothes. Something unsettling was running over and over in his mind, and the only way he knew to clear it was to sweat it out on a long run.

He was usually right about these kind of things. It was one of the main reasons he'd chosen the career path he had. He'd always had a knack for... just knowing. Especially when things were off or hidden. He'd always known when someone was lying to him or when someone was hiding something. Like Xtina had earlier.

But something deep inside him told him she was just hurt and confused.

As he set off on his daily run, he wondered why the local police had quickly closed the case and marked it an accident. The more he ran, the more certain he was that Christina's parents had been murdered. And that the local police were covering it up. So many questions ran through his mind. Did she know? Was she involved? He played over their conversation several times in his mind. She hadn't even hidden the fact that she was relieved that they were gone.

She'd never hinted at why, or what they had done to her to make her feel so bitter. As he rounded the corner, he stopped and took a deep breath. He hadn't meant to run to the bend in the road where her parents had skidded off into a large oak. But standing there with the sun just rising, he started questioning his skills.

The spot looked like a place that it would be easy for a car with bald tires to slide off the slick asphalt. But something still nagged at his gut. Why?

He walked over and touched the large tree with the gash in it. Instantly, his vision grayed and his knees went weak.

Behind his eyes, he witnessed a scene right out of a horror story.

A young couple stood over a large metal tub filled with steamy water. The couple's hands were clasped tight together, holding one another back. There, in the deep water, lay a very young girl with long flowing blonde hair. Her green eyes stared up at them in horror until finally, they closed in death.

He woke from the dream state when his knees hit the trunk of the tree. His fingers dug into the dirt as he threw up, emptying the tea and coffee he'd drunk that morning.

What the hell had that been? He took a moment to steady himself before he stood up again, making sure not to touch the tree or its large roots.

Taking a few steps back, he glared at the thing. If her parents had died there, did that mean they were still around?

He did a quick 180, his eyes moving over every tree branch, every bush, in fear. There was no way he was sticking around if more ghosts would be haunting his nights or days.

Then he remembered Xtina's words. *"She's not a ghost."*

If the lady in his bedroom wasn't a ghost, what exactly was she?

He turned around and started back towards the house at a slow pace, his mind racing over the scene that had just played in his head.

Was that Christina? Had her parents drowned her? He focused his mind on all the details he could remember, from what her parents had been wearing to what other objects were in the small room. He made mental notes of everything and was determined to jot them down when he returned back home.

He could probably chalk up the entire episode to lack of sleep. He only averaged five hours a night due to his... guest making an appearance each morning. That, or the fact that work had been stressful. Maybe it was because it had been a few months since he'd been out on a date.

His mind sharpened when he thought of Jessica Sorenson, the pretty brunette who worked in the local coffee shop.

He'd run into her the first week after he'd moved to Hidden Creek. He'd made it a weekly habit to stop by the Coffee Corner for coffee and muffins, and he'd asked her out less than a month later.

They had hit it off, something that had shocked them both. He'd had several relationships in the past, but nothing that felt as right as this one had. Jess had even commented on how crazy things had felt between them.

Then, two months later, it all fell apart. He wasn't quite sure what had happened between them, but the night he'd made plans to finally sleep with her, something changed.

Of course, they hadn't felt the change until after he'd unbuttoned her blouse and had a handful of those soft breasts of hers.

She had stiffened first, her eyes going wide, then he'd felt it. Her gray eyes had dimmed as she looked up at him. In his mind, they had morphed into something darker, something… greener. Her sandy colored hair had darkened to an almost jet black.

Jess had gasped, shaking them both out of the trance. Ever since that night, he'd avoided going into the Coffee Corner when he knew she was working.

His mind snapped to the fact that Xtina fit the description of his vision almost perfectly. Feeling a shiver up his spine, he quickened his pace, trying to shake the thought from his mind.

By the time he made it to the driveway, there was a sheen of sweat trickling down his back. The cold would be coming in the next month or so. The heat was actually something he loved about the south. Most people complained about the mugginess, but he actually lived for it. He loved the hot summer nights, the sultry mornings, and the cool evenings when the wind kicked up. He enjoyed the cooler winters too, just not as much.

When his little house came into sight, he smiled. The place was coming along. He still had the outside to paint, along with a long list of things to finish on the inside, but it looked a million times better than it had when he'd moved in. The yard was clear of debris, and the grass was starting to fill in where it had been bald. He'd spent a hefty chuck to lay down seed and fertilizer after clearing a lot of brush. By next spring, he had no doubt that his yard would look as nice as the big house next door.

Turning his eyes towards the giant home, he frowned. He'd never really given the massive house a second thought. The older couple had pretty much stuck to themselves. He'd never heard them screaming at one another, like his neighbors had in Atlanta.

They had a service that took care of the yardwork and maintenance around the massive yard so he never really saw Christina's father outside much.

In fact, the only time he'd actually talked to Christiana's parents was the day he'd moved in. He'd walked over and knocked on their door to collect a package of his that had been delivered to them by accident.

He'd briefly spoken to her father and had returned home less than ten minutes later. Their conversation had been short and friendly enough.

As he walked up the long driveway towards his place, he wondered how long Christina planned on staying. Or if she was thinking of moving into the house permanently.

He'd stopped himself before from looking into her background, but now that something nagged at him about her parents' deaths, and more important, the vision he'd seen, he had no qualms about punching her name into his system. He wanted to spend several hours learning all about Christina Warren or Xtina, as she liked to be called.

Jill Sanders

Chapter Three

After one of the worse night's sleep in years, Xtina decided to break her no caffeine rule and run into town for a strong cup of joe at the Coffee Corner. She needed the extra kick if she was going to make it through the day.

The small town of Hidden Creek hadn't changed that much except several new chain stores and restaurants had moved in. Coffee Corner was the only private business that still thrived, since it was easily the most popular. She second-guessed her decision when she saw the line of people waiting for their morning shot of caffeine. But her body and mind screamed for the liquid as soon as she smelled the sweet aroma in the air.

"Christina?" someone said from behind her and she cringed. She hadn't thought about the fact that people actually knew her here.

For the past few years, she'd really enjoyed being Xtina. She'd moved all over the States, enjoying her anonymity everywhere she went.

Pasting a smile on her face, she turned around and greeted Laura, one of her old friends from school. Over the next few minutes, she listened to the woman brag about her life; she had a wonderful husband, two darling children, and a big house on the outskirts of town. The part of her that was Xtina shivered, but Christina felt a slight longing and decided to ignore the jerk reaction to marry the next single man that walked through the doorway.

It was nice, however, to not have Laura jump all over her and try to hug her. She was thankful that most people in town remembered from her days in school not to touch her. Everyone except Mike, her mind broke in.

Why she'd thought about him now, at this time, was an enigma. As Laura continued to chat about her perfect life, the line slowly moved forward and Christina kept playing over the fact that her sexy neighbor with the hidden brown eyes was the only other person she'd ever met who could see the same things she could. She wondered if he felt what she felt too? Maybe that was why she hadn't been jolted with visions when he'd touched her. Maybe they had somehow crossed each other's powers out.

"Christina?" An excited voice came from behind her.

Xtina turned towards the counter to see Jess, her best friend from high school, standing behind the counter in a dark brown apron.

"Is that really you?" Her friend smiled and reached over across the counter towards her.

Xtina took a step back, knocking into Laura's chest.

As soon as she made physical contact with Laura, the vision came.

Laura was flat on her back, her long legs hoisted up around the shoulders of a blond man, who was easily five years younger than her. Her husband, a thick balding man, stood naked next to the bed, a video camera in his hands as he smiled down at his wife and the other man.

Xtina jerked forward, breaking the connection and desperately wishing for a shower as her stomach lurched angrily.

"Sorry," Jess said, rushing around the counter. "I'd forgotten," she whispered close to her, so no one else could hear. "Are you okay?"

Xtina nodded her head slightly. "I…" She thought about rushing towards the bathroom to be sick, but then cringed at the thought of standing in the long line again.

"Go, I think I can guess what you want. I'll have it waiting for you," Jess said, nodding towards the lady's room.

Xtina did rush this time, barely making it into the empty stall before losing what little she had in her stomach.

She was just washing up in the large stall, which housed its very own sink and mirror, when she heard two ladies come into the bathroom. She felt the shiver rush through her. Her knuckles turned white as she gripped the edge of the sink.

"Can you believe she's back? I mean, we all knew she'd come home for the funeral, but…"

"I know, and the scene she made." They both giggled. "No wonder she left in a hurry. I mean, making a fool of yourself in school is one thing, but as an adult." They both giggled. "You would have thought that she would have outgrown being a freak by now."

Everything after that was just a high-pitched sound in her head. Xtina waited until they were done washing up before she started breathing again. Then she waited another few minutes to make sure they had cleared out of the shop before exiting the stall.

She'd grown up listening to that kind of talk. Actually, she was used to much worse. She didn't hide because she was embarrassed. Not anymore. She hid because she wanted to avoid conflict.

Invariably someone would stand up to her. Someone would want to say their piece. After all, they were deep in the heart of the Bible Belt, and there were over three thousand bible-loving citizens currently living in Hidden Creek.

"Are you okay?" Jess asked after waving her over to a private booth near the wall of windows.

"Yeah." She glanced around. "Shouldn't you be behind the counter?"

"No, I'm on my break." Her friend's smile grew. "When did you get back?" Her smile dimmed. "I'm sorry about…"

She let the words hang, then when she felt she could, she nodded. "Last night."

"Are you staying?" Jess's gray eyes begged.

"I haven't decided yet." She reached over and took a sip of her coffee. It was exactly what she'd wanted. Her friend had always had a knack for knowing what people wanted. There was a large slice of coffee cake sitting next to her mug, so she pinched off a piece and stuck it in her mouth. The spicy bread hit her stomach and caused all of the fluttering to cease. "Thanks." She nodded towards the food.

"Anytime." Her friend leaned in. "What did you see?" Jess' eyes moved over to where Laura sat chatting away with another woman near the front door.

"Trust me, you don't want to know." She shivered at the memory.

Jess' eyes moved back to hers. Her friend was the only person she had ever confided in. Well, the only one she still trusted.

She'd never felt threatened or judged by the sandy-haired beauty that sat across from her. Nor had she ever felt the need to jerk away like she had moments ago. But, after five years away, she supposed it had become habit.

"I'm sorry... about earlier." Xtina's eyes focused on her hands wrapped around the coffee mug.

"Don't be. I should have remembered. Besides, it's been years since we've seen each other. I'm sure there's lots of new stuff up here..."—her friend tapped her skull and smiled— "that you don't want to know about."

Xtina met her friend's eyes. "You're wrong. I want to know all about you. Catch up. But I'd like to do it the normal way." She smiled. "I should have called."

Jess smiled and nodded. "Yes, you should have."

And just like that, they were back to the way they had been five years ago. No secrets, nothing to hide from one another.

Reaching out, she took her friend's hand and braced for the onslaught, pushing everything aside and focusing on only her friend's gray eyes. "I won't make that mistake again."

***

Mike walked into the Coffee Corner and

stopped dead in his tracks. There, across the room, was Xtina with her hand laying lightly on Jess's hand. They were looking into each other's eyes like long lost... lovers?

He almost burst out laughing then and there. Maybe the attraction he'd thought had been coming off Xtina last night had been all in his head. Or, maybe... he took a step closer and watched as Xtina dropped Jess's hand and Jess smiled. Maybe he was a dork and hornier than he thought. He chuckled when it became obvious that the ladies were nothing more than best friends.

Taking a very long deep breath, he headed over to the counter to order his coffee and a large cinnamon roll.

With his to-go cup in hand and the box holding his daily dose of sugar, he walked over to say hi. He wouldn't have normally done that, except the ladies made a point to wave him over.

"Hey," he said, standing at the edge of the table.

"Sit," Jess said, scooting over.

"I..." He looked between Xtina and Jess, about to make an excuse as to why he needed to run off, but in truth, he didn't have anywhere particular to be just yet.

"Go ahead, I'm sure she feels just as awkward as you do." Xtina nodded towards the empty spot.

His eyes narrowed as he looked at Jessica.

"Don't look at me." She giggled. "She walked in less than fifteen minutes ago and I've only gotten to say a few words to her so far."

He slowly sat next to Jess as he frowned. "I…"

"Easy." Xtina smiled. "It's a small town. People love to gossip about other people's relationships, especially failed relationships." Her eyes moved over to a rather pretty blonde sitting near the front door. He'd never met the woman, but noticed that she was watching him. She blushed and turned away when she noticed everyone at the table was looking at her.

"Oh." He set his coffee down.

"So, have you two officially met?" Jess asked, leaning forward until her thigh rubbed against his, sending a zing up his skin.

He scooted closer to the edge of the small booth and nodded. "Well, I guess you can call a cup of tea at three in the morning that."

"Oh?" Jess smiled and leaned on her elbows on the table. "Do tell."

Xtina sighed and took another bite of her muffin. He watched her lips as she nibbled the bread and felt his own stomach rumble. Opening the box, he took out his fork and shoveled a spoonful of sugar into his mouth.

"Wow, that looks amazing," Xtina said, breaking the silence. "When did you start selling those here?"

Jess giggled. "I started making them last year. I thought they would be too sugary for your taste." She took his fork from his fingers, broke off another piece, and handed it to Xtina. "Here, I'm sure Mike won't mind."

He didn't, but watching Xtina's lips close around his fork caused another kind of hunger to roll throughout his system.

"Amazing. You're a woman of many talents." Xtina gave a full, unhindered smile to her friend, and her green eyes changed to an almost emerald hue. It was quite possibly the most beautiful thing he'd ever seen.

By the time Jess scooted out of the booth when her break was over, he'd finished off his roll and coffee.

"I hope you got a few hours of sleep in," he said, following Xtina out the front door.

"Enough." She stopped just outside and zipped her jacket as her eyes scanned Main Street. "How about you? Did you get a few more hours in after…" She let her words drop.

"No, I never really do." He nodded towards the liquor store a few doors down. "Want to walk with me and help me pick out our poison for later?"

She smiled and fell into step next to him. "It's funny. I've been gone for almost five years and nothing really has changed. I mean, there are a few places that have a fresh coat of paint, some new signs, but underneath it all, it's just…" He held open the glass door for her. She was about to step in when she stiffened.

His eyes followed hers and landed on a man around his age behind the counter. The man's arms were easily double the size of his own and were fully covered in tattoos. His blond hair was spiked up, almost military style. Mike had talked to the guy a few times since living in Hidden Creek. He thought that the guy's name was Joe, but knew little more about him.

One thing was sure—nothing could drag Xtina into the store with that man in it. She took a step backwards and glanced around, no doubt looking for an excuse to leave him to his task.

"You okay?" he asked, reaching out and cupping her elbow. The slight touch seemed to jolt her out of the fear that had taken over her since he'd opened the door.

"Yes, I—"

"Listen," he interrupted, "I think I get it." He let the door shut and took a few steps towards the curb with her.

She closed her eyes and took a deep breath. "There's a reason I didn't want to come back to Hidden Creek." He waited until he felt her get herself back under control. "I'm not particularly excited to see everyone in town." Her eyes moved back towards the glass doors.

His hand brushed up her elbow until he was

holding her shoulders. Her eyes moved slowly up his hand until her eyes met his. "What do you want?"

She turned her body towards him, but she wouldn't look at him.

"I want…" The question loomed between them. "I want to be treated like I'm not crazy. I want to never see things, hear things, experience things that aren't normal. I want to leave this town behind without feeling the pull to return." Her eyes moved around the street once more. "To never run into people…" She turned her head back towards the building. "From my past." She trailed off and turned back towards him.

"I meant, what kind of wine?" His fingers had dug slightly into her shoulders but relaxed when she smiled and her eyes softened.

"Surprise me." Her eyes once more moved to his fingers still sitting lightly on her shoulder. "Something tells me you're good at surprises." She took a step back, breaking their contact, then turned and walked away.

He watched her disappear around the corner, then turned towards the shop, deciding it was high time he started asking Joe some questions.

Almost an hour later, he walked out of the liquor store feeling a little queasy himself. Something hadn't sat right with him when he'd approached the man about different kinds of wines lady friends would like. Joe seemed to know a lot. A lot more than your average meathead should.

The man asked all sorts of questions about what kind of lady friend he was buying for. If it was a date or a casual get-together. Somehow, Mike left the store feeling more like he'd been interviewed than the other way around. He had to admit, Joe was a smooth talker. It was a good thing that Mike wasn't the kind of person to answer questions. At least when he didn't want to.

Even though he braced himself, he knew the memory would flash up in his mind on the drive home. After all, how could you avoid seeing your best friend, who'd gone through hell with you, laying in a back alley, bleeding out, with your own service weapon still smoking?

He knew the shiver was coming and gripped the wheel harder when it racked his body. He felt sweat bead on his brow, trickle down his back. He didn't doubt that he'd lost most of his coloring too. His psychiatrist had said these were the classic signs of remorse and guilt, and to be expected when you've realized that the man you thought you knew wasn't who he'd been pretending to be.

Maybe that's why he no longer trusted anyone. He shook his head quickly. No, that wasn't right. There were still a few people he trusted. His parents, his brother... A pair of silver gray eyes and emerald green one's popped into his head. Shaking it again, he wondered why two ladies he hardly knew had been added to that very short list.

He pulled into his driveway. There was plenty of time before he would head over to Xtina's for dinner after her parents' funeral.

His mind rushed over how she'd looked that day. Her long hair had been pulled away from her face. She'd worn a dark skirt with a cream-colored blouse, which had only made her skin look creamier. He'd instantly wanted to test it to see if it tasted as good as it looked, which had been very awkward since he'd been sitting inches away from Jessie.

He knew Xtina had a full day ahead of her. He'd read in the local paper that her parents' funeral was being held at their church with the dinner afterwards at the house. But the paper didn't really say anything more.

His mind still raced over the possibility that her parents' accident wasn't... well, just that. His gut told him there was something more behind it, and after what happened to him last year, he'd learned how important it was to listen to his gut.

Jill Sanders

Chapter Four

There was nothing Xtina hated more than sitting in a church full of people. Except sitting in *this* church, full of *these* people. She knew almost everyone crowded in the small hundred-year-old white building. The church was one of the oldest in Hidden Creek and its congregation all believed it was the oldest because it was the most righteous. The building may have stood for a very long time, but its congregation and the people who ran it had all come and gone several times in just her lifetime.

The current pastor, a man in his mid-thirties, was new to her. She listened to him talk about her parents and preach his side-sermon and could see why the building was packed. He was a very good speaker. He kept the crowd entertained and added some emotion into what he said about her parents, and before she knew it, it was her turn to climb the stairs and stand in front of the microphone.

She'd toiled over her speech since being asked to speak a few days ago. What should she say? That she was grateful she'd escaped her parents' clutches years ago? That she believed her mother and father had been some of the worst parents known to man? Should she talk about the hours she'd hidden from them in fear? Or all the things she had to keep from them because of the punishment they would inflict or the methods they used in the name of God to cleanse her from the evil that had gripped her?

Taking a deep breath, she focused on the back of the room and started her planned speech about how they had impacted the lives of the people in town. How they had both been raised in Hidden Creek, met in grade school, fallen in love in middle school, gone on to marry shortly after high school, and settled down into their lives until the night they were tragically ripped from this earth.

When she sat back down, she noticed that a few more eyes in the audience were wet and realized that she'd done her duty as a daughter. She felt a jolt travel up her back and turned slightly as the pastor was finishing up his speech. When she noticed Jessie step in the back door, still in her uniform from the Coffee Corner, she felt a wave of relief flood over her. One person she could trust was now in her corner.

Jessie made her way towards Xtina after everyone stood up and started talking quietly.

"You okay, hun?" Jess started to touch her arm, but then held back.

"Yes, much better now that it's over."

"Sorry I couldn't make it to hear you talk."

Xtina almost laughed, but then glanced around the room and the somber people surrounding them. "I took it almost word for word from my mother's journal I found last night."

"Oh?" Jess sidestepped to allow an older couple to walk by.

"Later." Xtina tucked her arms into her jacket and hugged it tight. She hated this part. The part where she was supposed to stand by the door and shake hands with everyone while they sniffled and told her how great her parents were. "Stay with me?" Her eyes must have looked panicked because Jessie reached over and touched her arm.

"Sure." She dropped her arm quickly enough that Xtina felt nothing but love from her friend.

A little over an hour later, Xtina's head felt like it was going to explode. Her body needed a recharge and her mind needed a break. But there was a string of cars following her down the bumpy lane to her home and she knew no such break would happen for a few more hours.

The fact that Jessie's little blue car was right behind hers did cheer her up some. Then, when she pulled into the driveway, she noticed Mike standing on the front porch with a large brown paper bag in his hands. She couldn't stop the smile or the feeling that with him and Jess by her side, the next few hours would fly by.

"Hey," he said as she climbed the stairs towards him.

"Hi." She stopped right in front of him. He looked even better than last night and this morning at the coffee shop. He'd changed into dark slacks and a dark blue button-up shirt and had a black tie on. His dark hair was combed back and he'd shaved. She could smell the fresh scent of his aftershave, which almost caused her knees to buckle when he leaned closer to her.

"You look tired." His free hand reached out and took her elbow. "Are you sure you're up for this?"

It still jolted her to feel his touch without all the extra things flooding her mind. Her eyes traveled down to the spot where his skin touched hers. His fingers were long and strong looking. She'd noticed they matched the rest of him and felt her face heat.

"I'll survive, as long as that's what I think it is." She nodded towards the bag and watched a smile form on his lips and felt her heart skip a few pumps.

His hand stayed on her back as she unlocked the front door. Then it dropped away when Jessie started up the porch stairs.

"Hi." Her friend smiled and rushed over to them. "I'm sure glad I won't be the only one here to support Xtina."

Xtina felt stronger with the two of them by her side. She knew that Mike still felt awkward around Jessie but was pretty positive that would pass since Jessie had a way of making people relax around her.

Leaving them to talk just inside the doorway, Xtina walked into the kitchen. She needed to check up on the meals she'd pulled from the freezer and placed into the oven on low before heading out to the church earlier.

The house smelled like her mother's chicken casserole. Flipping on the coffee pot, she pulled the casserole out of the oven and checked it. It was perfect. Then she put in the three apple pies she'd found in the freezer and started setting out other items she knew she'd need.

Several of her mother's friends walked into the kitchen, all with their arms full of food and baked goods. Soon, the large kitchen was full of other scents and voices.

She avoided bumping into anyone by sitting down at the oversized bar top, after one of her mother's friends, Crystal, told her she looked too tired to help out. Jessie had come in and sat next to her, keeping her company while the women worked in the kitchen area and the men gathered in the living room.

She was thankful when Mike walked into the

kitchen almost half an hour later. He took her shoulders in his hands and leaned down to whisper in her ear.

"How's it going?"

She'd stiffened under his touch and when he noticed, he didn't drop his hands, but instead started gently rubbing her tired muscles, causing her body to vibrate. She was finding it harder and harder to keep her mind from wondering what else those hands could do to her.

"Once I get some food in me, I should be better."

"I think that they're almost ready." Jessie stood up. "Want me to get you a plate?"

Xtina shook her head and stood up, dislodging Mike's hands from her shoulders. "I can handle it myself. Thanks."

"Too bad there isn't some booze in the house," Jessie whispered, frowning at them.

Mike looked at Xtina. "Mike brought some… for later."

"Oh," Jessie said, then her eyebrows shot up. "Ohhhh." She dragged it out. "Wow, I guess things move fast…"

"Don't," Mike said, shaking his head. "Xtina asked…"

"No, I get it." Xtina could tell that Jessie was teasing, but she could also see a hint of hurt in her friend's eyes.

"I had hoped you would stick around too." She reached for her friend's hand. A shocked look replaced the hurt in Jessie's eyes when her palms touched hers.

Xtina hadn't braced for it, and the memory slipped in under her defenses.

Mike and Jessie were on a date at Shay Burbone's, a fancy restaurant at the edge of town. Then they were sitting outside her place as Jessie moved closer to Mike, their lips meeting for the first time. Heat and something else close to sparks spread through her friend. Next, they were on Jessie's sofa, arms and legs wrapped around each other as clothes were tossed aside.

Xtina could feel her friend's heartbeat spike as Mike reached for the clasp of her slacks, then, Jessie opened her eyes and... something was off. Mike wasn't... well, Mike. He was, but something was off about him. Instead of his longer messy hair, which she'd just enjoyed running her fingers through, it was much shorter, almost military. The soft smile she'd come to enjoy was gone, replaced by a hard line as he frowned down at her. Somehow, his nose had changed, too, it looked slightly crooked. Everything about him was... different.

When she blinked, Mike was back. This time, his soft full lips were frowning down at her.

"What the hell?" he asked, pulling back. "What the hell was that?" He shook his head.

Jessie jerked her arm free from Xtina's and the memory faded just in time for Xtina to see the room spin before everything went white.

***

Mike caught Xtina just before her head hit the countertop. Several ladies in the room gasped when they noticed that she'd passed out. He easily and gently picked her up and walked with her in his arms as Jessie led him up the stairs into what he assumed was her bedroom.

When he laid her down on the small bed, she moaned.

"I'll get her a cold washcloth," Jessie said as she disappeared through a doorway.

He glanced back down at Xtina just as her green eyes opened.

"There you are," he said softly.

"It was you, but it wasn't." She blinked a few times. "I…" She shook her head and he could see her eyes focus. "I guess I should have had more than a muffin to tide me over today."

He brushed a strand of her dark hair away from her face.

"Have you always had black hair?" He didn't know why he asked the question, but something told him he had to know.

"No." She shook her head slightly. "It's my way of rebelling." He watched her ample chest rise and fall slowly as she took a couple deep breaths. "That and this." She scooted up and exposed her upper left arm. An impressively colored tattoo covered most of her left shoulder.

"May I?" he asked, his fingers hovering over her skin. When she nodded and moved to sit up, he gently pulled down her loose sweater until he had exposed the entire piece of art.

It started at her collarbone, a black raven whose wings were spread out and had beady eyes red as blood. As his eyes slowly moved downward, he could see that the color of the bird's wings turned a shade lighter until they were purple, teal, blue, and hues of pink. When he looked at the piece completely, it no longer looked like a raven, but a beautiful black swan whose head was dipped down as if in a graceful defeat. The raven's eyes were no longer predominant, and instead, the swan's green eyes were the focal point.

"Wow," he said under his breath.

"Here's the water and some food…" Jess walked in, then did a double take. "Wow!" She set a tray of food down then rushed over to look at the art on her friend's body. "Where'd you get this?" Her finger brushed over Xtina's shoulder.

He watched as a shiver pulsed through Xtina's body. Quickly, Jessie's hand pulled back.

"Sorry." She frowned down at Xtina. "I didn't mean…"

Xtina reached for her hand. "It's okay, I'm just tired and hungry."

"I brought you up a tray." She walked over and brought the tray to her. "You stay here. Everyone is helping themselves and then I think I can get them to leave early since you're not feeling well."

"I couldn't…" Xtina started to say, only to have him hold her in bed.

"Sure you can." His hands gently held her back. The shoulder of her sweater was still down, exposing the colorful skin. "Jessie can get everyone to leave quickly, then we can open the wine I brought. That is, unless you want to hang out with everyone downstairs." He felt her shiver and watched her eyes close.

"Not particularly," she said dryly.

"Good, then it's settled. I'll let you know when the coast is clear," Jessie said, then disappeared out the door, only to peek her head in again. "Don't start the party without me. The wine, I mean." She winked then shut the door behind her.

"I think she still likes you," Xtina said, throwing him off even more. He dropped his hands from her skin and tried to think of something to say. "Don't worry, she has mixed feelings about you that are causing her not to act on anything."

"Um." He felt his mouth go dry. "I like her… I

thought things were going well, until…"

"Yeah, I saw what happened." She scooted up in the bed, shifting the tray of food in her lap.

"You saw?" He frowned down at her, not sure he understood.

"Sure, I mean…" Her green eyes grew large, then moved slowly towards his. "I mean… she told me…" She blinked a few times and he could tell she was lying.

"Xtina." He stopped her from continuing. "Why are you afraid?"

"I'm not." Her chin rose up a little.

He chuckled softly at her. "The night I meet you, I tell you I see ghosts, then—"

"She's not a ghost," she interrupted, scooping up a spoonful of casserole and taking a bite.

"Right, so you say. So, I tell you I'm seeing…" Her eyes moved up to his, stopping the word from coming out of his mouth. "A woman, who is see-through and floating at the foot of my bed," he supplied, and Xtina smiled slightly and nodded. "And you act like it's no big deal. But I've watched you. Here and at the coffee shop. You cringe every time someone comes near you. Every time someone touches you, your eyes go misty and grow blank. Then you're racked with—for the lack of a better word—spasms. All of the color leaves your body and you look like you've got a massive migraine. What's going on? Are you sick?"

She laughed, a rich, full-bodied laugh that filled the room.

"You could say that." She took another bite and closed her eyes. "You know, my mother was sure a bitch, but boy could she cook."

He felt his own head spin at the turn of the conversation. "Christina…"

"Don't call me that." Her eyes darkened and the smile disappeared from her lips.

"Then don't avoid the subject," he demanded.

Her eyes narrowed. "No, I'm not sick. At least not in the traditional sense."

"Then what? Why *did* you pass out downstairs?" he asked again.

She pushed the tray aside, then crossed her arms over her chest. Since the sweater was still pulled down over her shoulder, her breasts pushed together with the movement. A wave of desire struck him hard and fast.

"I'm just tired. That's all," she insisted.

He waited as he forced his eyes to remain on hers instead of her beautiful breasts.

"I have a knack for telling when someone's lying. It's what made me a great cop and I know for a fact—"

"You were a cop?" she interrupted.

"Yes, but you're avoiding the conversation

again."

"Where? In Atlanta?" She uncrossed her arms and leaned towards him.

"Yes, I was on the lower side."

"For how long?" Her green eyes looking eager.

"Almost four years." He still felt the loss of the job.

"Why'd you quit?"

"Who said I quit? Maybe I was fired?" he muttered.

She shook her head. "No, you quit. I can see the sadness in your eyes."

"Why couldn't I be sad about being fired?"

She chuckled. "I guess you could say I have a second sight about these sort of things, too."

His chin went up. "Tell you what, you answer my questions, and I'll answer yours." He waited until her lips puckered in a slight pout. "Fair?" He held out a hand. Her eyes zeroed in on it until finally, she slowly reached out and took it in hers.

"Okay, ask." She tried to jerk her hand away, but he held it firmly.

"First question. Why are you afraid to touch people or have them touch you?"

Her eyes moved to their joined hands. "I'm a germophobe."

He chuckled. "Okay, new rule. I promise not to lie… as long as you don't."

She sighed loudly, then nodded. "I see things." His eyebrows shot up.

"Like our non-ghost?"

She waited, then slowly nodded. "And more. When I touch someone, I can see… their memories."

He felt his skin goosebump over. "All of them?" His hand tightened in hers.

"No, just what they're thinking about at the moment."

He dropped his hand from hers and she leaned back. "Now you're afraid of me." She crossed her arms over her chest again.

"No…" he started to say, only to have her eyes snap to his.

"I thought you weren't going to lie, as long as I didn't."

He shifted slightly. "Fear isn't the right word."

"What is, then?" She waited.

"Concern."

"That I'll know all of your secrets?"

Shaking his head, he stood up and walked towards her window. There, in the dying light of the day, he could see his home in the distance. He'd left the front porch light on, so that he could

68

find his way home later.

Already, several cars had pulled out of the long driveway and he knew that soon the house would be empty once more.

"No, for putting anyone through what I had to go through," he said under his breath.

She'd moved without him knowing and when she spoke again, her voice was right behind him.

"What have you gone through?"

He turned to her. "Don't you know already?"

She shook her head slightly, her dark hair falling over her shoulders. "I can't…" She took a deep breath. "It seems that I can read everyone but you."

Jill Sanders

Chapter Five

"What do you mean?" Mike asked, his back towards the window. The sun was setting behind him, giving him a halo ring around his entire body.

There, she thought. She'd finally told someone else. She credited him for not running away in fear, but when he'd dropped her hands, part of her heart had broken off. But now he'd told her he wasn't afraid she'd know everything about him, but that she'd have to experience what he'd gone through.

"Was it something that happened that caused you to quit the force?" she asked, purposely avoiding his question. When he just looked at her, she crossed her arms over her chest, determined. "I answered one of your questions, it's only fair that you answer one of mine."

"Okay, yes," he said quickly. "Now, what did

71

you mean when you said you couldn't read me?"

She smiled and took a step closer to him. "Yes is not a full answer." She stopped right in front of him and his dark eyes hardened with desire. She enjoyed the way he'd looked at her skin, her tattoo, until Jessie had walked in. Her body had instantly responded to his desire. Now, she was almost shaking with want for him.

"Okay, yes, something happened to me on the force that caused me to quit." When he opened his mouth to ask his question again, she stopped him with a slight shake of her head and her eyebrows arching. "Fine, I was put into a position by my best friend and partner that could have easily led to my death. So, I shot Cameron, almost killing him, and saving not only myself but the city." He smiled and she couldn't stop herself from smiling back at him.

"Kind of like Batman? Was it a dark rainy alley?" she joked, but when his smile fell away as he nodded, she rushed over to his side.

"I'm sorry." Her hand went to his shoulder as his arms wrapped around her waist.

"I don't like to talk about it." His eyes met hers. "Now, answer my question."

"I… I don't see anything when you touch me." Her eyes moved to the spot where her hand rested on his shoulder. "You're a blank spot." Her eyes moved back to his. "You're the only one that this has ever happened with." She laughed and took a step back. His hands easily dropped away as she walked over to the window and looked out. "You know, it's funny. My entire childhood was one big punishment because I knew things about people I shouldn't have. I saw things…" She turned to him. "And now that I've found someone I can't read; it scares the shit out of me."

He chuckled as he took a step closer to her. "Does anyone else know? Besides your parents, I mean."

She dipped her head. "Jessie found out in fifth grade."

He smiled back at her. "And she's still around."

"Yes." She didn't realize she was crying until he reached up and gently brushed the tear from her cheek.

"I knew I liked her for a good reason."

Xtina couldn't stop the smile. "Everyone likes Jess."

"But not everyone likes Xtina?" he said and her smile fell away.

"No, Christina was the freak." She wrapped her arms around herself, leaning back against the windowsill. "My parents spread the news around town that I had a delicate skin condition and would break out in hives if anyone touched me." She closed her eyes remembering the pain that had caused her. All of the teasing, all of the names she'd been called. But she supposed it was better than the truth coming out.

"They were trying to protect you." His words were like a bucket of ice dropping on her head.

She tensed up and looked at him. "They were embarrassed of me. They thought I was a freak. They believed I had the devil in me. They ran to their God, demanding he fix me. They tried everything known to man and church to rid me of these…."

"Powers?" His head tilted to the side as he watched her intently.

She nodded slowly. "They tortured me." She raised up the right sleeve of her sweater and exposed the thin white lines that ran up and down her arm. "They bled me, burned me." She turned her wrist until he could see the circle marks from the heat. "They…"

"Drowned you." His dark eyes had turned red. His jaw was set in a strong line. If she didn't know better, she would have sworn he was having a vision of his own at the moment.

"Mike?" She took a step towards him, her fingers gently touching his arm.

"No!" He jerked away, then turned back towards her. "Tell me!"

She waited until she noticed his breathing steady, before nodding slightly. "Yes, they purified me with holy water."

His burst of laughter echoed in her room. "You mean they drowned you and revived you?"

74

She nodded. "Yes, that was part of what they thought was needed."

He turned away from her then and stared out the window. "The last car has left." He turned back towards her. "I'd better—"

She stopped him. "Don't. You promised to have a drink with Jess and I."

She could feel the tension leave his body at her touch. "I would have killed them," he said under his breath. "You were just a child."

A slight smile crept onto her face. "You did have a vision?"

His dark eyes closed, just as Jess walked into the room. "They're all gone." She held up the two bottles of wine. "I'd say getting drunk is in order." She tapped the bottles together.

Xtina reached down and took Mike's hand in hers as she followed Jess downstairs.

"Later," she whispered as she sat next to him on the front porch. "I'll want to hear what you saw." He nodded, then took a drink of his wine.

Jess leaned against the front porch railing and watched them. "Are you going to tell me what you saw?" she asked, after they had emptied an entire bottle.

"No." Xtina laughed and kicked the swing into motion again. "Are you going to tell me why you guys didn't continue dating?"

She watched as Mike and Jess exchanged looks. They both shook their heads and answered at the same time. "No."

"Then it's settled. Some secrets are better left unsaid." She held her glass up and clicked it with theirs.

At that exact moment, there was a bright flash from the three glasses. The fine crystal shattered in her hand as a wave of power spiked through her bones. Her eyes went dark until she could only see a ring of dim light coming from far above her head.

She could hear screaming and realized she was floating in water—deep water, cold water. It was too dark to see anything, but there was a foul smell to the air. Hands reached out to grab her, but she fought them off, pushing them away until she felt herself sinking deeper into the darkness.

"Xtina!" someone shouted. She felt her body shaking and when she opened her eyes, she could see Mike hovering over her. Instead of waiting for her to respond, he turned and started shaking Jessie.

Instantly, worry filled her. Her friend was laying on the front porch, her white blouse covered in dark red wine as she twitched about. Her gray eyes had rolled to the back of her head and she was saying one word over and over again as Mike tried to shake her awake.

"Byron. Byron. Byron."

***

"Who the hell is Byron?" Jessica asked, almost half an hour later. They had newly filled plastic cups of wine and had gathered around the fireplace. She'd lent Jess a sweater and was soaking her friends blouse to get the wine stain out.

Jessica had a thick blanket wrapped around her, as did Xtina. They were both huddled together on the sofa, while Mike stood in front of the fireplace.

"We thought you would know," Xtina said.

Jess shook her head. "I don't know any Byron." She turned to Xtina. "Do you?"

"No, I know a few Bryans, but no Byrons."

"Okay, but that doesn't answer my question," he broke in. "What the hell happened to us? One minute we're saluting, and the next I wake up in a puddle of wine with the two of you convulsing at my feet."

"Did you see anything?" Xtina asked under her breath.

"No." Worry flooded him. "Did you?"

Her eyes moved to his. "Yes, but it wasn't…" She shook her head slightly. "I mean; it wasn't about any of us. At least I don't think any of us have drowned in a dark lake with the moon overhead."

"No," Jess supplied.

"Not me either," he added.

"Tell us exactly what you saw," Jess said, reaching out for her friend but holding back slightly.

As she ran through her story, he became more worried.

"Why did your vision affect us?" he asked once she was done talking.

"I... I don't know. Nothing like that has ever happened before."

"Can she see her?" he asked, nodding towards Jess.

"I don't know." Xtina looked over at her friend, as she bit her bottom lip. "I've never told Jess about... her before."

"Who?" Jess asked, sitting up slightly. "Who is her?"

Mike walked over and took Jess' hand in his, then tugged her up and repeated the process with Xtina. "Up for an experiment?"

Jess smiled. "Oooh, I've never been asked to have a threesome before," she joked.

Mike burst out laughing. "I wish. Maybe some other time." He turned and looked at Xtina. "You up for this? You've had a pretty crazy day."

"She's never been anything but kind to me. Besides, I told you, she doesn't scare me."

"Okay. You might want to put on your shoes and jackets. We'll walk to my house." He held out Xtina's jacket and waited until the ladies had put on their shoes and jackets before holding the door open for them both.

"What's this all about?" Jess asked as they made their way across the yard.

"You'll see." He glanced down at his watch. He had an alarm set for the same time every night. "We're a little early, but I assure you, it's worth the wait."

When they entered his house, he could already tell there was energy in the air. Something wasn't quite right. As Jess shut the door behind her, Xtina turned to him.

"Something's different." She reached for his hand.

He took her hand, then reached for Jessie's and walked back towards his bedroom. The three of them sat on the edge of his bed in silence.

"What are we waiting for?" Jess whispered.

"Her," he and Xtina said in unison.

"Her who?" Jess whispered, sounding very impatient.

"My ghost," he answered, only to have Xtina tug on his hand. "Okay, not a ghost…"

He glanced down at his watch and waited silently as the minutes ticked by. When the hand

79

reached a quarter past one, a white film started to form in front of his eyes. His hand tightened on Xtina's and he glanced over to see that she was watching the form slowly appear in front of them. But when he looked towards Jess, she was glancing around the room like she'd rather be anyplace but in a dark room with two crazies who were seeing a ghost.

"You don't see her?" he asked Jess.

"Who?" she whispered back. "There's no one here."

He turned his head towards the figure and jumped when the dark eyes glared back at him.

"No, don't. Look deeper," Xtina said right next to his ear. "See the pain. The loneliness. The betrayal."

With her words echoing in the room, the dark eyes of the woman before him shifted. Soon, they were as gray as Jessie's but full of sadness and sorrow. The eyes moved between Xtina and his as she hovered over the floor, her form dissipating right below her knees.

"There," Xtina said, pointing to the woman. "Jess, do you see her?"

"I don't see anything. Are you guys punking me?" She stood up and walked in front of the figure, crossing her arms over her chest.

"Seriously?" Mike reached for and grabbed her back down on the bed since she was pretty much standing through the figure. "You don't see her?"

"No!" Jess almost yelled it. "There is no one here. What am I missing? Why can you see her and not me?"

Mike turned towards Xtina with the same question running in his mind.

When the woman finally disappeared, he released the breath he'd been holding.

"She's gone," he said, releasing his hold on Jess.

"Okay..." Jess stood again, crossing her arms over her chest. "Spill. Everything."

"I think I need another drink." He walked out of the room towards his kitchen. He pulled out his bourbon and threw back a shot quickly.

"Wow, tell me you're in the process of remodeling, because if not... yuck," Jess said, stepping into his living room.

He chuckled. "Of course. It's a work in progress." He turned and assessed his own house. There was no flooring down in the living room. His kitchen had a temporary countertop held up by two saw horses and the kitchen sink was just a bucket of water with a hose he could turn on and off with the flip of his wrist. "I remodeled the bedroom and bathroom first." He nodded back towards his room.

"You've done wonders already," Xtina

remarked.

"If you say so," Jess added dryly. "So?" She turned to her friend, waiting.

"I've seen her my entire life," she supplied.

Jess's eyebrows shot up. "Who?"

"The woman." Xtina shrugged her shoulders. "That Mike is seeing too."

"She's in her late teens…" He held up a finger and quickly disappeared down the hallway towards his office. Pulling out the file from his desk, he returned to the kitchen and set the folder on the countertop. "Here, everything I know on the gho— woman," he corrected. "Sorry, for almost a year I've thought of her as such, but after tonight… I'm not so sure."

"Why?" Jess asked. "What changed your mind tonight?"

"I'm not sure that ghosts can be selective of who sees them."

"She's not a ghost," Xtina said.

"Okay, you've still not explained how you know that." He turned to her as Jess looked through his file.

"Because… I touched her once."

"And?" he asked before it dawned on him. "Oh…"

She nodded. "Memories. A flood of them. They

were garbled and confusing, but… not from a dead person."

"How would you know the difference?"

"The dead don't… I can't touch their minds," she said matter-of-factly.

"Okay, let's put a pin in that for a moment," Jess remarked, causing him to chuckle. "So, tell us what her memories were full of." Jess held up his sketch of the woman. He wasn't an artist, but he'd taken his time and had drawn a pretty good likeness, or so he thought.

"They were all mixed up. Jumping around like she was trying to show me too much at once. She was in love with a boy, then there was a big party. She was dressed in white, like she is now. They were holding hands and walking through the woods, then she was…" Xtina stopped. "Oh my god!"

"What?" He rushed over to her side. "Are you okay?"

"It was her. She was the one…"

"When? What?" Jess and Mike asked at the same time.

"I saw her… She was the one drowning in the dark water with the sliver of the moon overhead."

"So she is dead?"

"No." Xtina frowned at him. "That wouldn't make sense." The room was silent for a while.

"Well," Jess broke in, causing him to jump slightly, "it's been fun kids." She glanced at her watch and whistled. "And I've got to be at work in about five hours. So, I'm heading home to get a few hours of sleep." She turned to Xtina. "Walk me back to my car?"

Xtina smiled and nodded. "Sure. I hope we're not creeping you out with all this." Xtina bit her bottom lip.

Jess walked over to her and hugged her lightly. He noticed Xtina had braced for the slight contact. "You always creep me out, but I still love you."

Xtina chuckled, then turned to Mike. "Are you going to be okay?" She glanced back towards his room.

"I'll be fine, but I'll walk you both back." He closed the file and walked over to open the door. Once more, he noticed the shift in the house. After the woman visited, things felt calmer.

They walked in silence back to the big house, which was almost completely lit up. After Jess drove away in her car, he stood on the porch and turned back to Xtina.

"Are you going to be okay?" He nodded towards her house.

"Yeah. I'll be fine." He wanted to move closer to her, gather her in his arms, but leaned back against the stair railing instead.

"What do you think it means? That she can't

see the woman?"

Xtina shifted her shoulders. "It could mean lots of things. The woman might not want Jess to see her. Or, she could be afraid to show herself to other people."

"What if it means that we're connected. Somehow?" He threw his thoughts out there, something he'd felt since first seeing her last night outside his window.

"Connected?" she asked. He did move to her this time, wrapping his arms around her slim waist. She tensed slightly, but didn't push him away.

"Let's just try an experiment," he said softly before dipping his head down to trap her lips beneath his.

Jill Sanders

Chapter Six

Whatever Xtina had expected of the kiss before, it paled in comparison to when Mike's lips touched hers now. She'd felt power her entire life. Power from the living, from the unknown, from the departed, but nothing could have ever prepared her for the power that came from the simple touch of Mike's lips.

Instantly, her entire body was on fire. She was sure that if she looked, sparks would be shooting from her fingertips and toes. He must have felt something to, because he broke the kiss too quickly. When her eyes fluttered open, he was looking down, and his eyes had gone huge as they scanned hers.

"That was… something," he said softly.

"Yeah," her voice squeaked. She was having a hard time catching her breath and wished her heart would settle back down in her chest.

"I… Okay, this is going to sound weird, but has that ever happened to you before?"

"That?" She shuffled her feet. When he nodded, she sighed. "Mike, I've kissed men before."

He chuckled. "I didn't doubt that." He moved closer to her. "I'm talking about the surge of power."

"You felt it too?" she asked, feeling stupid. She always assumed that she was the only one who ever felt… well, anything. Ever.

He dipped his head and pulled her closer. "Yeah," he said under his breath, then nudged her chin up until their eyes met. "Is it always like that for you? With other men?"

Her mouth had gone dry, so she just shook her head slightly as an answer.

"Good," he said before dipping his head again and brushing his lips over hers once more. She moaned and leaned into him.

No, it had never been like this before. Yes, there was power here, but more important, there was the wonderful silence she felt with him. She'd had to mentally shut out the memories of every man she'd been with before. With Mike, all she felt was her own memories, her own thoughts, her own desires.

It was wonderful.

Even though Mike was keeping the kiss soft, his hands moved around to her back, holding her tight against his hard body. She enjoyed playing her fingers over each cord in his back.

He was lean, like a runner, with long narrow muscles that ran down every part of him like a boxer. She'd never had the pleasure of enjoying someone so built before and desperately wished to explore even more of him.

But, all too soon, he was pulling away and softening the kiss. "You don't know how bad I want to come in and explore this more with you, but…"

She rested her forehead against his. "Too soon?"

"Yeah," he whispered against her skin. "Are you sure you're okay?" He pulled back and looked her in the eyes. When she just looked at him, he chuckled. "You did pass out twice today."

"I'm fine." She felt her face flush. "Besides, it's kind of a normal thing with me."

His eyebrows shot up in question. "Does that happen each time?"

"No." She shook her head. "Most of the time I'm prepared."

"So, you only pass out when you're not prepared?"

"That, or I get sick."

His fingers tightened on her arm.

"Go, I'll be fine." She smiled. "Besides, I need some sleep. I'm heading into Stockbridge tomorrow to visit my grandmother."

His eyebrows shot up. "Your grandmother lives in Stockbridge?"

"My parents put her in a home a few years back."

"That's a pretty long drive." She felt him move closer.

"Not as long as the drive from Colorado." Her smile slipped.

He was silent for a while. "I'd like to see you again."

She held in a chuckle. "We do live close."

"So you're sticking around?" he asked.

The question jolted her. For as long as she could remember, she'd hated Hidden Creek, hated the people who lived there. But ever since she'd left, she'd felt the call to return. Now, with the two people she hated and feared the most out of the way, was there any reason not to stick around? At least for a while?

"I haven't decided yet." She stood up and wrapped her arms around herself. "Thanks for bringing the wine."

He nodded, then took her hand. When he brought her fingers up to his lips, she felt a wave run down her arm directly to her heart.

"See you around." He smiled, then turned and started walking home.

Xtina walked into the house, making sure to lock the door behind her. She watched Mike's dark shadow disappear across the yard but it had nothing to do with making sure he got home safe. She loved watching the man move.

Okay, so maybe she'd gone too long between dates. Or, maybe it was the fact that, with him, she wouldn't get all the extra baggage of having to block memories from her partner.

As she climbed the stairs, her fingers trailed over the sturdy banister and her eyes wandered to the faded pictures along the wall.

When her eyes landed on one of her grandparents, she sighed. It had been almost eight years since she'd seen her grandmother. The last time she could remember was when the woman had stood up to her parents on her behalf. Shortly after, they had moved her out of the room down the hall from hers and more than fifty miles away to a nursing home.

Changing into a pair of yoga pants and a tank top, she crawled into bed and remembered the last time she'd seen her grandmother.

She'd been sixteen and desperately wanted to attend a dance at the school. Her parents had forbidden her from doing any extra activities.

Jessie had begged her to join the volleyball team with her, but her parents had forced her to attend nightly bible study classes instead.

Her grandmother had been so determined to get them to allow her to attend the dance that they had fought. It was the first and last time she'd ever heard her grandmother raise her voice.

From that moment on, Xtina had a new respect for the older lady. She'd never stood up for her before. Not the many times her parents had punished her for being different or when she'd been sent to her room with no food because she'd had a vision when holding hands to pray over the meal. She'd skipped a lot of meals. So much so, that she'd been a very skinny and weak child.

She had always dreamed that her grandmother would sneak food to her on those occasions, but her grandmother never had. Instead, she'd remained silent. Almost like it had never really happened. Which, in Xtina's mind, meant she condoned her parents' actions.

But she was still family and Xtina knew she had to visit her and make sure the woman was well cared for. After all, she would be paying the bills to the retirement home soon.

She cringed inwardly as she turned over in bed. She dreaded going through her parents' papers in her father's downstairs office. She couldn't imagine they were in debt; the house had been paid for generations ago. Both of her parents' cars were so old, she doubted the bank had loaned them any money for them.

Her father had worked down at the hardware store all his life. She'd seen enough of her parents' childhoods through their minds that she probably knew them better than they knew each other. But, in all the memories, nothing had ever hinted as to why they had treated her the way they had.

She must have drifted off since a few hours later she was jolted awake by someone knocking at her front door.

"Sorry," Jessie said, holding up a cup of coffee and a brown bag. "I bring peace offerings." She wiggled the bag on the other side of the glass door.

"What are you doing here so early?" Xtina yawned and opened the door.

"I felt so bad for bailing on you last night. I didn't mean to get freaked out." She handed over the coffee and opened the bag. "I made these yesterday, but we can heat them up really quick. I have about…"—she glanced down at her watch—"half an hour before I have to be into work."

"Come on back." She took a sip of her coffee as she walked into the kitchen. "This is good." She frowned at her cup. "Why is this better than what you sell at the shop?"

"Because I made it on my very own maker." She smiled. "You will have to get one for yourself." She glanced around the kitchen. "You need to start someplace in order to bring this kitchen into the current century."

"I don't normally drink this much coffee." She frowned down at the cup, but when the warm liquid spread through her, she couldn't hold in a sigh. "But, I suppose buying a coffee maker would be nice just in case I want a cup once in a while. Not to mention a microwave." She groaned when she pulled out a pan and flipped the oven on.

"So." Jess sat down at the bar and watched her put the rolls in the oven for a few minutes. "How did it go with Mike after I left?"

"Fine." She turned back towards her friend. "Are you sure things didn't work out between you two?"

"Yeah." She saw a shiver run through Jess. "It's hard to explain. I mean…" She rested her chin on her palms. "I'm *very* attracted to him and I think he was with me, too."

Xtina nodded slightly. "I can see that. After all, you are pretty hot stuff."

Jess laughed. "Okay, so there is mutual attraction."

"Then what happened?" Xtina already thought she knew, but wanted to hear it from her friend's mouth before saying anything.

"I'm not sure. I mean, one minute we're going hot and heavy and the next second… fizzle." Jess made a diving noise as her hand swooshed downward.

"So? You wouldn't feel weird if I told you he kissed me last night?"

Jess caused Xtina to jump slightly when she squealed. "Of course not!" Jess leaned almost all the way out of her seat. "So?" She sat back. "How was it?"

Xtina rolled her eyes. "You should know."

Jess chuckled. "Of course I know, but I want to hear you say it."

"Wow," she said under her breath, remembering the kiss and what it had done to her. "Just… wow."

"I couldn't agree with you more." Jess sighed and rested her chin back on her hands. "I was sure hoping that it was a fluke. It should be against a law… that amount of passion in just one kiss. But I'm glad you two are getting along."

"I don't know. I mean." She walked over and leaned on the counter. "I haven't experienced this with someone before." Jessie's eyebrows shot up. Xtina paused. "I can't read him."

Jessie's chin dropped. "You mean; you can't see into his mind?"

Xtina shook her head.

"Wow. What do you think that means?" Then her friend gasped. "Is that why you two can see the ghost and not me?"

"She's not a ghost," she replied almost automatically. "I don't know. Mike seems to think so, too."

"Okay, if she's not a ghost, then what is she? Mike seems to be convinced she's an apparition."

"Like I said, she has... memories."

"Wouldn't ghosts?" She leaned over a little more, moving her feet up under her. "I mean; they were once people."

Xtina felt a shiver run up her spine. "No, they only project emotions."

Jess leaned back. "What aren't you telling me?"

Just then the timer chimed on the oven. She turned around to pull out the rolls before they burned. When she set one in front of Jessie and took the seat next to hers, her friend turned to her.

"Go on." She motioned for her to continue talking.

Xtina had hoped that the conversation would end, but she noticed the determined look in her friend's eyes.

"Fine." She threw up her hands, but held up a finger to take a bite of the cinnamon roll first. "Mmm, you're going to have to share this recipe with me."

"You're stalling," Jessie said, shoveling a bite into her mouth. "Okay, yes, I will, since these totally rock!" Xtina laughed. "Go on." She waved her fork at her.

"My first memory, I was four. I was sitting up in my room, crying. When my mother came in to comfort me, she asked me why I was crying. So, I told her it was because the man standing at the window was sad that his son wouldn't be coming home from the war." She watched Jessie shiver, then reach for her cup of coffee and swallow a large drink.

"Go on." She almost whispered it. "What happened?"

"My mother glanced towards the window, then turned back to me. Her eyes were huge, so I thought she saw him, but instead, she rushed from the room and brought back my father. They spent the entire night praying over me. They made me memorize the Lord's Prayer that night and made me say it over and over again. I was four. I barely knew how to spell my name at the time. Every time I would see the man at my window, they would have me say or write down the prayer. Sometimes I would write it out until I had blisters on my fingers."

"I remember seeing your hands covered with blisters," Jess said. She reached out but pulled her hand away quickly. "Sorry. What happened to the old man?" She glanced towards the stairs.

"He's gone, along with the woman in the attic and the children in the field."

Jess shivered and almost dropped her cup. "What happened to them?"

"Remember the time we snuck to the local library after school?"

Jessie's eyes narrowed. "That was on St. Patrick's Day, right?"

"Yes, while you were talking to the boys, I was researching a book I'd heard about. One on how to get rid of them. It was pretty rudimentary, but after a couple tries, they disappeared."

"Do you still see them? Others I mean?"

"Sometimes, but I learned that they only show themselves once you're connected to the property."

Just then Jessie's phone chimed. "Damn, I've got to go. How about dinner tonight?" she asked, standing up and shoving the rest of the roll into her mouth.

"Can't." Xtina stood up too. "I'm going to see my gran today. I might not be back until late."

"Tomorrow night?"

Xtina nodded. "I'll bring something…"

"No, you won't, we'll go out. You know where I'm at?"

"The same place?"

Jessie nodded. "Good, you can pick me up. Sometimes I think I'll be there until I die."

"You could move out here with me."

Jessie laughed and glanced around. "Without a microwave, TV, or… well, internet? No thanks."

"I do plan on changing all that… soon." She looked around and thought about all the changes that needed to be done to the place to make it more modern.

"Ask me again after you're done." She turned to go. "Oh, if you need anything…" She smiled. "You've got a big strong neighbor to help out."

Xtina laughed as her friend slammed the front door behind her.

Jill Sanders

Chapter Seven

Mike hung up the phone and smiled. It was sure nice to know that his checking account balance had just been increased by a few thousand dollars. He'd actually liked working for Bartle LLC and was hoping to make it a more permanent deal. After all, they were one of the leading government liquidators in the south. And as such, each of their new employees and prospective buyers had to go through a rigorous background check, which fell into Mike's expertise.

After logging off his computer, he stood up and stretched. He'd been sitting down for the past few hours and could use a run, but decided to spend his pent-up energy knocking out the flooring in the living room and kitchen instead.

He loved hard work. Work that was dirty and sweaty. Something that made his muscles scream for a few days afterwards. Something that would help him sleep through the night.

After the other night, he assumed that his visitor would leave him the hell alone. Instead, she seemed even angrier than before. Except when Xtina was with him. Then, she seemed more tolerable.

He pulled on a pair of old sweats, Velcroed on his knee pads, and got to work. Several hours later, his phone beeped with a new message.

-Being sent overseas again. – E

He replied quickly to his brother.

-Can you tell me where?

-Nope, being shipped off early next week. Won't be back for a few months.

-Did you tell the folks?

-Yup, mom cried, dad gushed with pride.

-When are you going to end their pain and settle down?

-When are you?

-Let me know when you're back. Love ya man.

-Back at ya.

He hated thinking of his brother stuck in some hole somewhere until he was called on. But fresh out of school, they had both decided the military was the best choice for them. Mike's career had only lasted two years, then he'd moved on to the police force. Ethan had signed up for another four years. His brother lived for his job, and if Mike had to be honest about it, the country needed his brother as much as Ethan needed the military.

But every time Ethan was sent off on some secret mission, their mother would worry and their father would stress until he was back in the States, safe and sound. Usually, Ethan being away meant that he'd be hearing from his folks on an almost weekly basis. Which wasn't such a bad thing. Especially now, since he was off the force and could actually sit down and enjoy the phone calls.

Sure enough, less than half an hour later, his phone rang.

"Hey, Mom," he answered after seeing her name and photo pop up on his screen.

"So, you heard?" she asked.

"Yup, he texted me about half an hour ago."

"Well, did you ask him if he's going to stop all this soon?"

"Yes."

"And?" she finally said after a moment of silence. He held in a chuckle.

"He asked me when I'm going to settle down right back."

"Well?" She was beginning to sound impatient.

He could just see her, standing in their kitchen, her arms crossed over her chest, glaring across the room at the back of his dad's head as he watched the game.

"As soon as I find someone who can cook like you, I'll marry her on the spot." He knew that would soften her up.

"Well…" He could hear her smile. "Don't wait too long, dear. Almost all of the good fish have already left the sea."

He chuckled. "All it takes is one." His mind snapped to Xtina and his eyes moved towards the large windows in his living room. It was too dark out to see if her car sat in the driveway, but he did notice that the house was dark, which meant she was either asleep or not home yet.

He'd watched her come and go, yesterday, when she'd gone to visit her grandmother. He wondered how the short trip had gone. He also spent a few hours today wondering if he should stop by later tonight, but ended up telling himself that if she wanted to see him, she knew where he lived, too.

"You aren't listening to a word I'm saying." His mother's tone broke into his thoughts.

"I'm sorry, Mom. I've been working on putting the hardwood floor in for the past few hours."

"Oh? How's that going?"

"So far, so good. Actually, I should be done

104

sometime tomorrow."

"That's wonderful dear, send us some pictures when you're done. When are you going to get the kitchen done so I can come down there and cook you a proper meal?"

"After the floor and the baseboards are in, that's the next on my list."

"Good. Maybe we'll head your way when Ethan gets back," she said worriedly.

"Don't worry about him too much. He is a big boy."

"I worry about you both, all of the time. It's my job."

He smiled and shifted the phone. "Well, at least don't worry too much. After all, his squad is one of the best around."

"Yes, that's true. I'm so very proud of both of you. How's your business going?"

For the next twenty minutes, he filled his mother in on his latest client. When he happened to mention his neighbors dying in a car crash and their sexy, mysterious daughter returning home, his mother flooded him with a million questions.

What was she like? Was she married or single? What did she do for a living?

He realized that was something he'd yet to ask her himself. He knew what her profile said online. For the past two years, she'd run a little shop on

105

the outskirts of Idaho Springs as a psychic, where tourists stopped to get pizza and ice cream and have their palms read. Before that, she'd lived in Arizona in what appeared to be a Humanist Society. The community boasted that free thinkers of all types were welcome and that education was given freely by experts in various fields. They discuss the arts, books, social events, politics, technology, religion, and more. The one statement by the leader, William Ray, that had caught his eye was about supernatural beliefs and how the society had a progressive philosophy on the supernatural. The man looked to be a few years older than him and he wondered what gave the man so much knowledge in the area, since he couldn't find anything more on him.

He'd researched as much as he could about the society and still questioned what Xtina had been doing there. She didn't have an online presence tied to them, which meant that she'd broken the ties as soon as she'd moved on. He wondered if she'd found what she needed there or if it had just been some big joke, like he assumed the place was. Still, she'd spent almost an entire year living there.

Before that, she had moved around so much, he'd lost track of her several times. He knew she'd been in Seattle, L.A., and even Houston. But, everything in between was just a blank.

He'd planned on asking her more when he saw her next and asking some of the questions his mother had asked him about her.

After convincing his mother that he would invite Xtina out for dinner soon, he cleaned up and headed into town for a quick burger.

The little café in town had switched owners late last year and had changed its name to Café 23, in honor of the highway it sat directly on. They'd gone from a greasy diner to a family friendly joint that had some of the best milk shakes and burgers around.

After cleaning up a little, he climbed into his truck and headed out. He noticed that Xtina's car was not in the driveway and wondered where she had gone to all day.

When he pulled into the busy parking lot of the diner, he smiled when he noticed Jessie and Xtina sitting in a back booth, their heads bent over a large book as they chatted.

The bell chimed over the door and both of the ladies glanced up at him. Jessie's smile was quick, but Xtina just bit her bottom lip when she noticed him.

"Evening, hun," Clara, one of the waitresses he'd been flirting with for the past year, said. She was easily as old as his mother and as frail as his grandmother, but he didn't mind. He liked the silver-haired woman. Maybe because she always gave him extra French fries every time he was in there.

"How are you tonight, Clara?" he asked.

"Oh, doing fine. Find yourself a seat, sweetie. We're hopping tonight."

"I'm going to join a couple friends." He nodded towards the booth.

Clara glanced over, then smiled. "Oh, looks like I've got some competition."

He chuckled. "You'll always have my heart…as long as you keep feeding me hamburgers, French fries, and chocolate shakes."

"Coming right up," she said as she glided away.

When he walked over to the booth, Jessie had moved aside so he could sit next to her. Instead, he sat next to Xtina, pushing her over slightly with his hip.

"I sat with you last time." He winked at Jessie. "Now it's her turn to get me."

Jessie laughed. "From what she tells me, sounds like you'll be choosing her over me all the time now." She leaned on her elbows and smiled at him.

He glanced over at Xtina. "Have you been kissing and telling?" He watched her face flush and thought the color added sex appeal to her beauty. He reached under the table and took her hand in his. At first, her fingers were stiff, but after he started chatting with Jessie, he felt her relax.

"So, you've put in the floor?" Jessie asked. "Was that what all that wood was sitting in your living room?"

"Yes, I have my kitchen cabinets in the garage. I'll be starting on those next."

"I'm not big on remodeling. They fixed up my apartment last year and I was stuck in a hotel for three weeks."

He chuckled, then turned to Xtina. "What about you? Don't you have plans for the big house?"

"Actually, we were just talking about that." She turned the book towards him and he noticed a page full of microwaves.

"I'd really like to heat food up in less than thirty minutes," she said, causing him to smile.

"If you need any help, I just purchased all new appliances for my place a few months back. I can show you the best deals and brands."

"Really?" She shifted, dropping his hand to flip through the pages.

"What is this?" He pulled the book from her. "Sears? You shop for appliances using a magazine?"

"It's all my parents had."

"Don't you use a computer?"

Jessie's burst of laughter caught his attention. When she tried to cover it with a cough, he asked. "What's funny? Computers are…"

"Oh, I use a computer, but our girl here, you see, her parents were a little backward thinking."

109

He turned to Xtina. "You don't own a computer?"

She shook her head. "Actually, I've never even used a computer before."

He almost laughed, but then stopped. "What about this?" He picked up her phone, which was sitting on the tabletop.

"That's just my phone."

He smiled and punched a few buttons, then frowned. "You don't have data?"

"Data?"

"You know?" Upon her blank look, he shook his head. "Okay, seriously?" He turned back to Jessie.

"Told ya." She smiled. "I've tried, but she just seems so... stuck."

"I can hear you, you know," Xtina said. "Besides, I always end up breaking something. I went to the library once to register my business name, and the whole row of computers almost burst into flames." He felt her cringe.

"I'm sure that's an exaggeration," he said.

"No, it's not. The fire department showed up," she added, causing Jessie to giggle.

"If you want, come over tomorrow and I'll help you order everything online."

She bit her bottom lip. "I might explode your

computer."

He smiled. "I think I'll risk it."

She shrugged, just as Clara showed up with his burger, fries, and shake.

"That looks good," Jessie said. "I'll have what he's having."

Xtina shook her head when Clara asked if she wanted the same. "No, I'll just do the fries and shake."

"Light eater?" he asked her after Clara left.

"I ate before I left the house. Besides, red meat doesn't sit well with me anymore."

"So…" Jessie leaned over and took one of his fries. "Xtina was telling me all the different places she's been."

"Oh?" He turned slightly towards her, reaching once more to take her hand in his. He wanted to get to the point where she didn't flinch when he touched her.

"She lived in L.A. for a few months." Jessie sighed. "I've never been to a big city before."

"Never? What about Atlanta?"

"That doesn't really count." She snuck another fry from his plate.

"Want some?" He tipped his plate towards Xtina, who took two and nibbled on them. "So, where else did you travel to?" he asked.

"Here and there." She shrugged her shoulders.

"Colorado." Jessie ticked off on her fingers. "Washington, Oregon, Utah, Nevada… Oh…" She sat forward, excitement rolling in her gray eyes. "Tell him about winning the car in Vegas."

"What?" He turned towards her again. "You won a car?"

She smiled. "At a blackjack table. My hybrid."

"You won that car?" He nodded out the window where her car sat on the street out front.

"Yes. What they don't tell you is that you still have to pay the taxes on it. So, I ended up paying a few thousand out of my savings, but when you think about it, a brand new hybrid for a couple thousand isn't bad."

"I'm taking you next time I go to Vegas," he joked and wondered why Arizona hadn't been on the list she'd shared with them.

"I don't think I'll ever go back there." He noticed her shiver and turn her eyes downward. "Too many people."

***

There were too few times in her life she could look back on and say she'd truly enjoyed herself. This was quickly becoming one of them.

She couldn't remember laughing as hard in her entire life as she had in the last half hour. She'd even felt herself relax when Mike reached out and touched her or took her hand in his.

Sure, she was a little uncomfortable with answering all the questions Mike and Jess had for her, but near the end, Jess had turned it around and had flooded Mike with questions.

She found out more about him in a normal way, which, she'd quickly found out, wasn't all that fun after all. She'd wished several times to be able to reach over and find the answers for herself.

By the time her plate of fries was gone and she'd finished the last of her shake, she was hoping the evening wouldn't end. But Jess had let out a few yawns and mentioned how she was working the morning shift again tomorrow.

"I'll walk you out." Mike took her hand and helped her out of the booth. She was so comfortable with him touching her that she didn't even flinch at his touch.

"You know, I was thinking about something…" Jess started walking out the doorway, but then dropped away and stared straight ahead.

Xtina looked in the direction and felt her entire body tense. Her hand dropped away from Mike's as she watched Joe walking casually towards the diner.

"Well, well," he said once he got closer to them. Just the sound of the man's voice caused her skin to crawl. "Look who's back in town. I'd heard you'd come back."

"As opposed to the rat who never left town," Jess observed, crossing her arms over her chest.

"Careful, girlie, I haven't seen any moving vans outside your place." He didn't even spare Jess a glance. "Heard about your folks," Joe added, using his massive shoulders to block the pathway to her car.

She nodded as she wished the cement would open up and swallow her.

"I have to say, you're looking a lot better than I imagined." His eyes ran up and down her, causing her skin to continue its crawling.

Now she wished she'd worn an old sweater and jeans instead of the cute outfit she'd chosen just in case she'd run into Mike. Who, to her new horror, she realized was standing right next to her. She felt her entire body begin to shake with fear and anger over the possibility of what was going to happen next.

"If you decide you're bored, why don't you give me a jingle, you know." His eyes turned to Mike and Joe's smile grew bigger. "For old times' sake." He winked at Xtina, then skirted around them and disappeared into the diner.

"You know, my first impressions of people are usually dead on," Mike said, taking her hand in his once more. He turned to her until her eyes met his. "I had him pegged for an ass the first moment I walked into the liquor store."

She heard Jess chuckle, but nothing could

penetrate her desperate need to escape.

"Hey," Mike said as he brushed a finger under her chin and forced her to look at him once more. "Don't sweat it. I have a few skeletons' in my closet I prefer to keep there too."

"Joe isn't just a skeleton," she started.

"He's the devil," Jessica said. "Well, now that all the fun is over, I really do need to get home." She yawned again, causing Xtina to hold back one herself.

"See you," she said and waved to her friend as she walked down the street.

"Should we walk her home?" Mike asked.

"No, she'll be fine." No matter what she thought of Hidden Creek, it was still the safest town in Georgia. Maybe even all of the South.

"Well, the least you can do is let me walk you to your car." He tugged on her arm lightly until she fell into step with him.

"Actually..." She stopped and leaned against her car. "I was hoping you'd allow me to follow you home." When his eyebrows rose, she quickly added, "So you could help me order my microwave."

He smiled. "Sure. Tired of doing things the old-fashioned way?"

She rolled her eyes. "You've no idea." She groaned.

Chapter Eight

$\mathcal{M}$ike felt Xtina's breath float over his skin and couldn't stop himself from imagining how it would feel in other places. It had been way too long since he'd enjoyed the feeling of a woman's breath on his bare skin.

She leaned closer to him as he surfed the web for the best appliances. They had already picked a microwave and were now looking for a single-cup coffee maker.

"I have this one." He tapped the screen. "I like it fine enough."

"Hmm." She frowned. "How is it for tea and hot cocoa?"

He shrugged. "I'm not a big tea maker, but I

have made hot chocolate in it before." He showed her another screen. "See, it has a setting for it."

"Okay." She bit her bottom lip. "It's a little more than I wanted to spend."

"Well, last time I was in Atlanta, I noticed they were on sale."

"No, I'll just bite the cost. I don't know when I'll get back into town and I'm becoming accustomed to enjoying a cup in the morning."

"You know; you could always knock on my door. I'd be happy to share a cup with you in the morning." He turned slightly and smiled at her. "Better yet…" He wiggled his eyebrows, earning a smile and a chuckle from Xtina.

"You do make a persuasive argument." She smiled. "Thanks for the offer."

"But?" He ran a finger down her arm.

"Just like my house, I'm kind of old fashioned." He watched her eyes turn sad. "Besides, as witnessed earlier, my relationships don't always turn out the way I'd hoped."

He turned his chair towards hers. "So, why did you and douchebag go out?"

She closed her eyes for a moment. "Believe it or not, there was a time when Joe was one of the nicest kids in town."

He whistled. "That is hard to believe."

"Yeah, I guess now." She leaned back. "But, in tenth grade..." She shook her head.

He sat up slightly. "Was he your first?"

"First?" She frowned. "No." She shook her head. "Yes, I mean..." She actually blushed. "He was the first boy I tried to go out with. If that's what you mean."

"Sex," he said plainly, then chuckled when she made a face.

"No, I didn't sleep with Joe."

"That's good to know."

"Why?" She tilted her head and frowned slightly.

"Because when we're finally together, I'd hate to think of you with him."

"Mike—"

He closed the distance and laid his lips over hers gently.

It still shocked him when he felt the zing up his body as their skin touched, but this time he'd braced for it, much like he imagined she braced herself each time she touched someone.

Her hands moved up and gripped his shirt in her fists as he played his tongue over her lips. He allowed his fingers to explore her soft skin and enjoyed feeling goose bumps rise wherever he touched her.

When she pulled back slightly, he watched her eyes focus.

"I..." She shook her head and swallowed. "It's so hard to fight what's between us." She leaned her head against his forehead and closed her eyes. "Order me the coffee maker. I better go home now before... before." She chuckled.

"Stay. I know...I know what you think, but stay anyway."

She shook her head quickly. "No, maybe soon. But not tonight."

Seeing the fear and determination in her eyes, he nodded and then turned back to the computer screen and clicked a few buttons, placing her order. "How about I walk you home?"

"No, I can find my way." She stood up. "Thank you... for helping me." She nodded to his laptop.

"Thank you." He smiled. "For not blowing it up." She chuckled and then turned towards the door.

He watched her walk towards her house and smiled when the lights turned on inside. He sat back down at his screen and knocked off a few items before bed. He hadn't realized he'd stayed up so late until he felt the chill on the back of his neck. Turning around, he watched the brightness appear just a few feet away.

He'd never seen her appear outside of his room before. This time, he noticed there was no anger,

119

only sadness in her eyes. She glanced towards the bedroom and for a minute, he felt like he owed her an apology. Then he shook that feeling off when he realized he was about to explain to a ghost why he was working late. Not a ghost, he told himself and held in a chuckle.

She disappeared as quickly as she showed up and this time, he actually felt an emptiness when she was gone.

He shut his computer down and crawled into bed, but he couldn't sleep. His eyes were glued to the ceiling as his mind filled with Xtina.

The next day, when his phone buzzed, he rolled over and answered his mother's call. Glancing at the clock, he realized he'd slept most of the day away.

"You sound tired," she answered. "Didn't you get any sleep?"

His brain was too foggy to register who he was talking to, and before he knew it, he had answered.

"Yeah, I guess between the ghost and Xtina, I was too preoccupied to sleep."

"Ghost?" The tone in his mother's voice woke him up and he groaned.

"I mean…"

"What ghost?" His mother covered the phone and called out to his dad. "Charles, Michael is seeing ghosts."

"Mom, no, I wasn't awake." He sat up and rubbed his hands over his face and thought about pulling out his hair. "It was a dream."

"What's all this about seeing ghosts?" His dad was now on the line. He closed his eyes and wished desperately for a cup of coffee.

"I was half asleep."

"Was it the ghost or a woman that kept you up?" his mother asked.

He stopped himself from answering, "Both," just in time.

"A woman," he replied, hoping to divert the conversation.

"Would this be Xtina?" his mother said slowly.

"Yes,"

"Who's Xtina? What kind of name is that anyway?" his father asked.

"She's my neighbor, and her name fits her perfectly."

"Well"—his father's voice got a little louder— "sounds like we have perfect timing for our trip."

"Trip?" He felt his stomach kick in. "What trip?"

"The one we're planning for next month to come see you."

He tried to think of a million excuses but knew

that they wouldn't listen to any of them anyway.

"When?" he finally asked.

"Around the tenth," his father supplied.

"That should give you plenty of time to finish your kitchen."

He groaned outwardly as he looked around at everything that still had to be done.

"Roseline, don't pester him about the kitchen. I'm sure he's working as fast as he can," his father broke in.

"It's not pestering, Charles, I'm just mothering."

He listened to his parents argue for a few minutes as he walked into his kitchen, hit the button on his coffee maker, and poured a hot cup. When he glanced over at the house next door, he wondered if Xtina was up yet.

"He's not even listening to us," his mother broke in. "No doubt thinking about Xtina."

He shook his head. "I did mention that I didn't get enough sleep last night."

"Yes, yes." He could imagine his mother waving him off with her hands, the move she made all the time when dismissing him. "We'll let you go, we just wanted to let you know about our plans."

After hanging up, he decided some more sleep wouldn't hurt. Unfortunately, his phone rang and he spent the next few hours working on a new project. Getting paid was better than sleep. Besides, he was hoping to save up enough money to get the next phase of the house done soon.

By the time he hung up from the last call, his stomach was growling and he had a slight headache. He dug around the kitchen and threw together a ham sandwich. Shoveling it and a handful of chips into his mouth, he decided he needed a few hours of sweat to clear his mind of Xtina.

Since his folks were going to be making an appearance in a few weeks, he figured the first place to work on would be his guest room. It only needed a fresh coat of paint and new hardwood flooring laid down, which he figured he could finish by dinnertime if he worked fast enough.

The paint went on smoothly and before he knew it, the walls were covered in a warm gray/blue. He touched up the white baseboards and crown molding he'd put in a few weeks before and then started hauling in the boxes of wood for the flooring. Strapping on his kneepads, he got to work laying the planks. He had a saw set up out back and took trips to cut the measured boards until he was on the last board.

Glancing outside, he realized he'd worked faster than he'd expected, since it was still daylight out. He straightened and rolled his shoulders and stretched all the kinks from his back just as his stomach growled again.

This time, though, he decided a cold sandwich wouldn't cut it, and he was just about to reach for his keys to drive into town when there was a knock at his door.

When he opened the door, a smile spread on his face. "Hey," he said to Xtina, who was standing on his front porch looking very sexy in a pair of tight jeans and a low-cut silver sweater that hugged her just right.

"Hey," she said back, her own smile matching his. "I was thinking…" She glanced into his house briefly before her eyes settled back on his. "Would you come somewhere with me?" His eyebrows shot up in question. "I have this theory," she finally added. "It won't take long."

He tilted his head. "I was just about to get some food. Could we grab something on the way?"

She smiled and nodded. "Sounds good to me," she said after her stomach growled softly.

"I'll just get a jacket. It looks like it might rain later." He nodded up to the dark skies.

She followed him inside when he motioned for her to come in. "So, how is the remodel going?" When he turned to her, she smiled. "I heard the saw."

"Come have a look for yourself." He took her hand and walked towards the back, stopping just outside the guest room door.

"Wow," she gasped. "You did this all today?" She walked into the room as he leaned against the doorjamb.

"Yeah, call it a need to work off lack of sleep."

She turned to him, worry flashing behind those green eyes of hers. "Did she keep you up?"

He smiled. "No." He moved closer to her. "Thinking about someone else did." His hands took her hips and he pulled her close until his lips covered hers. He'd been starved for the taste of her again. He felt her melt against his chest. Her fingers dug gently into his shoulders as she relaxed into the kiss. When he felt her shiver, he pulled back slightly, not wanting her to feel how much he wanted her.

"It still gets me," she said softly as she rested her forehead against his chest. "Not being able to see anything." She shook her head.

When his stomach growled again, she chuckled. "Later." She shook her head and took a step back, glancing once more around the room. "There's a lot I'd like to do to my place." She turned to him. "Ever consider getting paid for this?"

He laughed. "I don't think my back would survive." He rolled his shoulders again, feeling the kink between his shoulder blades.

"I can help with that." Her fingers fidgeted for a moment. "Later."

He smiled. "It's a date." He took her hand again

and this time walked her to the front door. "Where were you thinking of grabbing some food?"

"How about some pizza?" she asked as they walked towards her car.

"Sounds good." He opened her door for her, then rushed around to the passenger side and climbed in.

"So," he said when he settled in the seat, reaching over and taking her hand, "our first date." He smiled and winked at her and watched her cheeks turn a nice shade of pink.

***

Xtina parked in O'Riley's Pizza parking lot and wiped her sweaty palms on her jeans. Michael made her feel nervous. She didn't know if it was because she couldn't read him or if it was the pure desire and lust she felt when she was around him.

Either way, her body had a way of acting strange when he was around. She watched him dart out of her car and rush around to her side to open her door.

She'd never really "dated" someone before. Sure, she'd gone on dates, but looking across the table in the noisy pizza place, she doubted that's what this was. Mike wasn't a "one date" kind of guy.

Her mind flashed to Jessie, and she felt her heart skip.

"So," she said after they had ordered a large

veggie pizza, "are you ever going to tell me what happened between you and Jess?"

She could tell that he didn't want to talk about it, so she nudged slightly.

"I mean, I kind of saw…" She bit her lip. "From Jessie's point of view."

He shifted in the booth. "What did you see?"

"The night you went back to her place."

"And?"

"How everything was hot and heavy… can I just say, wow, by the way." She smiled when he chuckled. "Then…" She made a fizzle sound and leaned back.

He blinked a few times, then leaned back when the waitress delivered their drinks. She'd ordered a seltzer water while he'd gone for a cold beer.

"I guess you could say I had a vision."

"Of?"

"What did Jessie say?" he asked, taking a drink of his beer. She could tell he was stalling but knew that he had his reasons.

"Just that it didn't work." She shrugged. "It's like there's this…"—she motioned her hands in a circle— "secret between the two of you."

"No, no secret." He took her hand. "Just weirdness." He chuckled. "For lack of a better word."

127

"What kind of weirdness?"

He closed his eyes and leaned back. "You're not going to let this go are you?" She shook her head slightly. "One moment I was kissing her, then... I wasn't."

"What do you mean?"

"I was... kissing someone else."

"Who?" She waited, watching his dark eyes focus on hers.

"You," he said softly.

"I... I don't understand. How were you kissing me?"

"We were there, on Jessie's sofa, and I looked down at her. Her brown hair turned darker, her gray eyes turned green, and her lips..." His eyes moved to hers and she had to swallow when she saw pure desire behind them. "It was you. I hadn't met you, but it was you."

"Okay," she said after she swallowed again, then reached across the table and took a gulp of his beer. "Wow." She shook her head.

"Yeah, wow. What did you see from Jess?"

She opened her mouth to tell him, but then the pizza arrived and the conversation changed. She was thankful since it was a little strange to tell Michael something intimate from her friend.

When they finished their pizza, they piled back into her car and headed to the edge of town.

As she drove, she thought about her visits to her grandmother. Each trip was harder and harder to deal with. Not that the old woman was a saint, but Xtina had always had a fondness for the woman. And seeing the rate at which she was declining was wearing on her.

Before this trip, the last time she'd seen her grandmother, she'd been a very frail woman in her early seventies. Now she was pushing eighty and looking at least twenty years older. She wasn't just frail anymore, she was rickety.

Her grandmother could no longer walk and was confined to a wheel chair. Her hands shook and she was so thin that Xtina thought that if a big wind blew through, the woman would topple over.

But her mind was sharp as ever. She talked to her about her parents, about how she'd been raised.

Xtina had asked why she'd gone along with all of their craziness and had been highly disappointed at her answer.

"Well, dear, we did what we thought was best. You were always a very odd child."

After that, Xtina had avoided touching her, since she didn't want to experience any history she might get from the contact.

It had been hard to refrain from comforting the woman, up until that point.

"What are you thinking about?" Michael broke into her thoughts.

She glanced over quickly, then turned down the road she wanted. "My grandmother. I've seen her two times."

"And? How is she?"

"She's fine."

"Are you going to keep her in Stockbridge?"

"Yes," she said, knowing she had to tell him more. "She's where she belongs." She felt a shiver run down her back.

"What's wrong?" He reached over and took her hand.

"She knew and, worse, she actually justified the way they treated me."

He was silent for a while. "I'm sorry."

She shrugged, trying to rid herself of all the negative thoughts that were flooding her mind.

"I have an uncle who killed his wife," he blurted out.

She glanced over at him as she pulled to the side of the road. "What happened?" She leaned so she could look more closely at him.

"He came home to find her beating their kid, so he pulled her off of the child and she hit her head against the stove. Killed her instantly."

"How terrible." She reached over and took his hand. "What happened to him?"

"Oh, he's living in Jersey with his seventeen-year-old daughter. My cousin was ten at the time and testified that the abuse had been going on for years. The marks on her body had been enough to corroborate his story. Actually, he's a pretty cool guy." He shook his head. "Just got a bum rap for a few years. But now he owns his own shop downtown and has made a pretty good life for them. Even found a pretty awesome woman and married her last year." He smiled.

"Why…" She shook her head. "Why tell me this?"

He leaned closer to her. "You had a bum childhood, but look at you now." He reached up and brushed a strand of her hair away from her face. "You're an amazing person who is kind and full of amazing things. Your parents were asses." She chuckled, causing him to smile. "But you don't let it affect you. That's pretty amazing in my book."

"Thanks." She leaned over and placed a soft kiss on his lips. "I've never had anyone deliver a pep talk to me before."

He chuckled. "Now, are you going to tell me why we're out here"—he glanced out his window to the darkness— "in the middle of nowhere?"

She nodded, her smile falling away slightly. "We're here to see a ghost. A real one this time."

Chapter Nine

Mike's entire body went on guard. "A…"

"Ghost," she broke in and smiled slightly, sending more shivers down his body.

"I…" He tried to think of a million reasons to not get out of the car, but when she cocked her head slightly, he knew the challenge was on. "Lead the way." He got out of the car, but before he could open her door, she was beside him.

"This way." She had brought a flashlight and took his hand as she led him through thick bushes.

The farther into the trees they went, the more his anxiety rose. Finally, they entered a clearing and the sound and smell of rushing water hit him.

"What is this place?" He glanced around. The moonlight was bright enough to see, so she switched off the flashlight.

"This is Starr's Mill Waterfall." She nodded to a dark building he could see across the way.

"The make-out place?" He glanced down at the few parked cars, which no doubt had steamed windows. Everyone in town knew that the old mill was the perfect place for teenagers to go "watch the submarine races." He turned to her, his arms going over his chest as he smiled down at her.

"Yes," she said, not giving him any attention.

"You know, if you just wanted to…" His words fell away when he felt it. He spun around so fast that he almost toppled over the edge of the cement pathway they were standing on. Her arm reached out and steadied him.

There, hovering less than a foot away was… well, a ghost. A real one.

Xtina was right. This one looked… different. Instead of a figure of a woman, this was just a puff of smoke with long brown hair. He felt his entire body go on guard and he pushed Xtina behind him.

"It's okay," she said in a soft voice. "Here." Xtina walked around him and took his hand. Instead of just holding it, she raised their joined hands until their fingers brushed the mist. He jerked his hand away quickly, but she just took it again. "Trust me." Her eyes met his and he was

133

powerless to deny her.

This time, when their fingers touched the mist, an onslaught of emotions inundated his mind. Pain. Sorrow. Happiness. Fear. Love. It all hit him at once, like he was a child uncertain of how to control his emotions.

"Try to focus," Xtina said softly into his ear. "See past all the emotions."

He did as she asked and soon, there was only one emotion. Betrayal.

He dropped his hand, Xtina letting hers fall too.

"What happened to her?" He watched the figure hover over the water, as if permanently tied to the spot. Then he turned to her. "I thought you said you didn't know anyone who had drowned before?" He remembered the night at her place, the image she had described after that night when the three of them had… an episode.

"She didn't drown." Her eyes moved to the water. "It's her grave, not where she died."

"Where did she die?" he asked, wondering why he couldn't let it go.

"Over there." She nodded to where the cars sat. "Almost thirty years ago." She turned to him. "By her lover's hand." He waited. "Her husband was an ass, so she had started having an affair with one of her son's schoolteachers. They met here on occasion, but when she became pregnant, she demanded he leave his wife for her, promising to leave her husband. Instead of running away together, she ended up here." Her eyes moved to the dark water.

"And the teacher?" He drew her closer to him when he noticed her shivering.

"Lived a happy life until her body was discovered a few years back. Her husband had spent fifteen years in jail for her death, until forensic evidence proved him innocent. The teacher, Carl Simon, ended up killing himself a few days after her body was found. He left a note for his wife. He had been riddled with guilt and confessed to killing Beth."

"Then why is she still here?" he asked, looking at the mist once more.

"To see the happiness." She nodded towards the cars. "The love she never was allowed to have."

"Why don't you..." He waved his fingers towards her. "Do your magic and send her on her way?

She laughed. Not a little chuckle, but a full-blown laugh. "I'm not Samantha."

He tilted his head in question.

"You know, from *Bewitched*?"

He shook his head again.

"There are some serious holes in your knowledge of old television shows." She shook her head and took his hand, once again leading him down the pathway, only this time they were heading back towards her car.

"I haven't sent her on her way yet"—she glanced over her shoulder— "because she isn't harming anyone. Besides, no one else knows she's here." She stopped at the hood of her car. "And I think, underneath the hurt and betrayal, she rather enjoys where she's at. I get the feeling it's the first time in her... life, she's actually happy." She smiled.

He nudged her until her back was up against the side of her car. "Like I said, amazing." He leaned in and laid his lips gently over hers. He doubted he'd get used to feeling the spark that happened each time he touched her. Or the desire that welled up every time he looked at her.

His hands roamed over her hips as her fingers pulled his head closer by closing around his hair. When her nails scraped the skin along his neck, he felt his control slip slightly.

"I don't know how much longer I can wait," he said between breaths. He felt like he'd just run a marathon.

"I know," she said under her breath.

"Why wait?" he asked, pulling back and looking down into her green eyes. "What's the reason?"

She leaned back against the car and shook her head. "Right now, I can't think of one."

He smiled. "How about you let me drive?"

Silently, she pulled her keys from her pocket and handed them over to him.

***

Talk about nerves. Xtina thought she would get herself back under control by the time he pulled into his driveway, but instead, she felt even more nervous than when she'd handed him her keys.

She'd done a few really stupid things in her life, and she was starting to question if being with Michael would be one of them. There was no way she would be able to hide the way she felt about him if he took her inside. Normally, she would be able to mask her feelings by focusing on what the person touching her was feeling. But now. She closed her eyes and took several deep breaths as he shut off the engine. But before she had a moment to cool down, his mouth was covering hers in a kiss that had all those emotions she'd been so desperately trying to hide surface full force.

Her hands went into his thick brown hair, holding him closer until she felt her entire body shiver with desire. She didn't know if it was her own, or if she was feeling the desire that was clearly radiating from him. Either way, she knew she'd been a fool to question being with him. This was right. This was what should be happening. And the sparks between them were proof.

His hands moved under her shirt, brushing

across her bare skin, and she moaned with delight.

"My god," he groaned across her skin just under her ear. "I want you so bad." He trailed his mouth down to just above her shirt collar.

"Michael," she said as she leaned her head back against the headrest. Then she laughed when he tugged lightly on her shirt to expose more skin. His head jerked up and then his eyes met hers.

"Sorry," he mumbled. "Going too fast?"

She shook her head. "Not if we were inside." She nodded towards his front door.

"Right." He pulled away and quickly got out of her car, leaving the keys in the ignition. Reaching over, she shoved them in her purse and waited for him to open the door.

When the door opened, she reached her hand out and took his. At that same moment, there was a flash in her mind. Pain shot up her arm towards her temples. A blinding light flooded her eyesight until a new scene unfolded in front of her.

She was outside an old hotel, the one that looked like it was off of Highway 23. The place had been in desperate need of remodeling when Xtina had been a child. Now, it appeared as if it should be condemned instead.

Laura was there, reaching for the door handle to room number 18. When she opened the door, she saw her husband on the floor, his massive body slumped near the edge of the bed. Laura rushed

138

over to him, taking his shoulders and shaking them. When her fingers came back soaked in blood, she started screaming as his body rolled to the ground.

Leaning down, she listened for a breath, but didn't hear anything. She felt for a pulse with shaky fingers, as tears began to form in her eyes. Her mind had just jumped to the idea of calling for help when, from the corner of her eye, she saw a dark figure before everything went blank.

Xtina fell backwards against her car as her body convulsed. She could hear Michael yelling at her, but his voice sounded too far away.

Then she was being carried towards the house and she snapped free of the panic.

"No," she jerked, trying to break free. "I have to…"

"Get a drink of water." He set her down, none too gently, on his sofa as he walked over and poured her a glass of water. "Drink first, then tell me what you saw."

His face had gone completely pale. When she was finished drinking, he took the glass from her, making sure not to touch her fingers.

"Was it the alley?" he asked, soberly.

"Alley?" She shook her head, not understanding. "I…" Then it dawned on her. He'd been touching her. He assumed she'd finally seen what had happened to him that night his partner had died. "No, it's Laura." She stood up, feeling steadier. "I have to call the police." She reached for her phone, only to realize that she must have dropped her purse outside.

"Who's Laura?" He stood up and followed her towards the door.

"A... friend." She glanced over her shoulder. "She's in trouble."

"I'll drive." He reached down and picked up her purse from the front porch, where she'd almost absently stepped over it.

Taking out her keys, she handed them to him and then pulled out her cell phone. "The little motel off 23," she said, following him to the car. "Drive fast. I think someone's going to kill her."

He stopped, then turned towards her. "You stay here." He started to rush back to the door. "I'll get my gun." She jerked him to a stop.

"There's no time."

His sarcastic laughter stopped her. "What?" she said impatiently.

"You tell me that someone is at a motel room, trying to kill someone, and you want to rush in without a weapon?"

"Yes," she growled. "We have to go now." She felt a pulse in her skull and almost hunched over with the new pain. "Now!"

He shoved her back into the car, then sped out

of the driveway, spraying rocks as the car whipped around.

"Call the cops." He cursed when the car fishtailed slightly as they hit the main road.

"On it." She took out her phone and called. Suddenly, she realized she didn't know what to say. So instead of a long story, she lied.

"I saw a man hurting a woman at the motel on 23. Hurry, it looks like she's bleeding." She hung up and tucked the phone into her purse. She knew they would have her number and she would have to explain exactly how she'd seen all this from behind closed doors, but she figured she'd deal with it later.

By the time they pulled into the hotel, she was no longer getting anything from Laura and was pretty sure they were too late.

"There." She pointed to the door.

"Stay here," he growled out. He turned and looked at her. "I mean it." When she nodded, he jumped out of the car and knocked on the door.

"Housekeeping," he called out, trying the door handle, then he leaned his ear against the door.

She watched him take a step back and kick the door open with one quick motion. When he disappeared into the room, her heart completely stopped beating. Her eyes were glued to the front door, counting the seconds until he appeared again.

He moved over to her side of the doorway and motioned for her to roll the window down.

"What?" she asked, fear emanating from her entire body.

"I think you need to come in and comfort your friend."

"She's…" She swallowed.

"Alive. She has a pretty big bump on her head, but her husband…" He shook his head. "Come on." He opened her door and held out his hand. "Stay with her until the police arrive."

She nodded, then followed him inside. It was just as she'd seen in her mind. Her husband, Daniel, was laying just where she knew he would be. Only this time, she knew there was no way anyone could revive him.

Laura sat in the corner in an old green chair, crying into a towel while holding another bloody one up to her head.

When she noticed Xtina, her eyes closed. "I…" She shook her head. "I tried to save him."

"I know," she said, rushing over to her side. This time, she mentally prepared for the onslaught of emotions before she touched the woman to comfort her.

"We were supposed to meet." Her eyes met Xtina's. "For a date night." Xtina blocked the images she'd seen in the coffee shop. "I was late getting off work. When I came in…" Laura's eyes moved over to where her husband lay. "He was barely breathing."

"The cops are here," Mike broke in. The sound of his voice temporarily broke her concentration and she let down her guard as her hand lay on Laura's shoulder.

Images of Laura and another man flashed hard and fast in her mind. So much so that Xtina almost fell backwards, her hand dropping from her shoulder.

"What have you done?" she whispered, her eyes going to the other woman's.

"I don't know what you mean?" Laura's eyes darted towards the door. "I tried to save him," she repeated. "My husband was shot before I got here." More tears burst from her eyes and her voice rose slightly as the police walked in. "Then someone hit me over the head. He killed my husband!" She almost screamed it.

Xtina's eyes narrowed and she stood up straight. When she turned to the police, she met Michael's eyes and he must have read her thoughts.

"We should step out and let the police get to work." He took her arm and her mind cleared. "We'll be outside when you're ready for us to answer questions." He tugged on her arm until she followed him into the cool night air.

"She was in on it," she said softly. "She had her

143

lover kill her husband and then hit her over the head so it would look like she wasn't involved." He stopped her a few feet away and took her shoulders, then turned her towards him.

"You sure?" he asked. When she gave him a look, he sighed. "Yeah, I guess you are. Any chance you might know where her lover is or what his name is?"

She closed her eyes and then shook her head. "I've never seen something like this before without touching someone." He shook her head. "We were almost five miles away from Laura when I saw…" She tilted her head. "Give me your hand." She held out her own.

Michael looked down at her hand, then took it. Once more, she closed her eyes. Images started appearing slowly behind her closed lids. "He's at the gas station on the edge of town. He's cleaning the blood from his hands in the men's restroom."

Michael dropped his hand and rushed back into the room with the cops, one of which followed him out quickly. "What does he look like?" the police officer asked.

"Sandy blond hair, gray T-shirt, and dark blue jeans. He's got a scar just above his left eye and a tattoo of an eagle on his left arm."

"Stay put," Michael called back to her, then shocked her by jumping into the vehicle with the other officer and driving away in the police cruiser.

"I'll have a few questions for you in a minute."

The other officer, an older man, stepped into the doorway just as two more police cars arrived.

The next few minutes were filled with lights, sounds, and a million questions, most of which she didn't know how to answer. Instead of rambling on, like Laura was doing, she sat silently and sipped the water a paramedic had handed her.

By the time her phone chimed with a new message from Michael, she was almost shaking with worry for him.

-*I'm okay. We have him and are heading to the station. Can you pick me up here?*

-*Yes*

She had a million questions for him. She also wondered how she would answer questions about how she knew exactly where the guy was. And how she knew that he and Laura had murdered her husband together.

The older officer broke into her thoughts. "Miss, we'd like to take you down to the office for further questioning."

She held in a groan. She'd purposely never helped the police before because most of them didn't believe in mediums or people who "saw" things.

She knew she was a suspect when Laura locked eyes with her and her chin rose slightly as if to say, 'See, I got away with it and now I'm going to pin it on you.'

Well, the old Christina would have allowed it to happen, but Xtina was a different animal all together. A wild one that didn't care if she was labeled anymore.

"I'll follow you down there," she said in a clear tone.

When they arrived at the simple teal stucco building, Michael was standing out front talking to a few officers. The smile on his face told her that he was enjoying the conversation.

She parked in the visitor's spot and before she could open her door, he was there helping her out.

"You okay?" He took her into his arms.

"Yeah, you?" Her voice was muffled by his chest.

"Never better." He pulled back and smiled down at her. "You ready to do this?" His chin dropped slightly.

She closed her eyes and took a deep breath. "I can't hide it anymore, can I?"

A chuckle escaped his lips. "The cat's out of the bag now." He took her hand and started walking towards the building.

"Mike tells us he used to be on the force in Atlanta," the cop from before said as they approached. "Also tells us you've got some…"— he waved his hands in a fluttering motion— "powers." The two other police standing around them all watched her.

146

She turned to the one on the end, a chunky man who appeared to be in his late forties. When she held out her hands, he hesitated for only a moment before placing one of his own in hers.

She opened herself up to the images and tried to glean as much as she could.

"You're Terry Jefferson, born Terrance William Jefferson. Your parents were both killed in a botched burglary in Houston when you were fifteen, sparking your interest in becoming a police officer. You lived with your aunt and uncle, who took you in as their own and joined the force straight out of high school. You married your high school sweetheart and have two kids and three cats."

She took a breath and stepped back, then turned to the next officer, the older man, who just shook his head and put his hands behind his back.

"Too much junk up here..."—he tapped his head— "I want to keep to myself."

She smiled and inclined her head before turning to the last officer. It was the man who had been at the hotel before and had gone to the gas station. He was taller than Michael and appeared to be a few years older. He looked slightly familiar, but she figured it was just because she had seen him several times that night. His jaw was set and strong looking, yet his eyes carried softness and concern.

When she held out her hands, he smiled a sexy

crooked smile with perfect teeth and took them in his own hands.

They were larger, but remained gently rested in her own hands. The instant they touched, power shot up her arms and she frowned. Her eyes met his and she blinked a few times.

"You have a gift," she told him before images of the man as a child flooded her mind. "You never knew your birth parents and were adopted at a very young age." Her voice broke the silence surrounding them. "They raised you in Hidden Creek. Your adopted father was the police chief until he retired last year. You're hoping to someday take over as chief yourself." She dropped her arms and shook her head from the all the other information she'd received. He'd been blocking a lot, but she'd gotten past his defenses and found out as much as she needed, more than even he knew she'd gained about him. So much so that she knew she had to talk to him in private, after they settled the matter at hand.

"So?" she said after a moment of silence. "Do I pass the test?"

Terry mumbled. "Anyone in town could find out my story." He turned to them. "What?" he said upon receiving the looks. "It's true. All you have to do is spend a few days in Hidden Creek and you can find out anything you want about anyone." He shrugged.

She turned to him. "Your wife is pregnant with

148

your third child, your first boy." Her eyes met his. "Congratulations."

His bark of laughter filled the empty parking lot. "Lady, until then you had me spot on, but there is no way Kelly is pregnant again." He made the scissor's motion above his zipper and shrugged.

"Call her." Xtina smiled. "She's been dying to tell you." She turned and watched the man dig out his phone and take a few steps away. Then her eyes moved over to the first officer, who was still watching her. "You didn't *give* me your name." She wasn't sure he even understood that he had tried to control what she learned about him. Something in his eyes had her a little confused about the man.

"Jacob," he supplied as her eyes moved to his badge and she read "J. St. Clair."

"Jacob, when this is all settled, maybe the three of us could have some coffee?" She took Michael's hand in hers.

"Sure," he said, his eyes never wavering from hers.

Suddenly, everyone's attention moved back towards Terry, who returned to them, slight tears in his eyes.

"Well, she has my vote," he said, wiping a tear from his face. "Kelly just found out yesterday and was in the process of making me dinner so she could tell me tonight when I got off shift." His smile grew big.

Michael's hand squeezed her own. "Now that that is settled, maybe Xtina can fill us in on the details of what happened tonight."

All eyes turned to her and she knew that it was going to be a very long night.

Chapter Ten

There was little Mike became impatient about, but dealing with red tape was one of them. He'd never enjoyed that aspect of the job when he'd been a police officer himself and was finding it especially difficult sitting on the other side of the desk now.

They were interviewed in separate rooms, then put together and interviewed again. He knew the drill, but still, by the time everyone was done asking them questions, the sun was coming up again.

Xtina looked exhausted. She leaned her head on his shoulder and gripped his hand tightly.

Jacob walked over to them finally and smiled. "Looks like we're finally done with you two." He turned slightly as all three of them watched a female officer leading Laura into the back room, her hands cuffed behind her back as she glared at Xtina. The blood on her shirt had dried to a dark brown color. "The boyfriend finally talked," Jacob said, turning back towards them, "after you gave us the details about how the two of them had met on the swinger's site."

Mike stood up, stretching his legs and back, then turned and helped Xtina stand.

"How about that coffee?" Xtina asked Jacob. Her hands gripped his firmly.

Jacob glanced down at his watch. "I get off shift in half an hour. How about I meet you at the Coffee Corner?"

Xtina nodded, then tugged on Mike's hand.

"Are you going to tell me what that's all about?" He nodded back towards the building as they walked towards her car.

She glanced back over her shoulder, then back to him. "In half an hour." Her lips twitched slightly and he couldn't tell if it was a smile or a smirk.

He opened her door for her but stopped her from getting in and pulled her close. "I'm sorry the evening didn't turn out like we'd planned." He enjoyed her soft breath on his skin.

"Me too." She wrapped her arms around his shoulders. The night hadn't been a total loss, since he'd spent most of his time with her.

"We could always head back, take a long nap, then…" He trailed his mouth over her soft lips. "See what happens next."

"Mmm, coffee first." She pulled back slightly. "Then we'll see." Her smile caused his heart to jump in his chest.

By the time they arrived at the Coffee Corner, his stomach was growling uncontrollably.

"Looks like we're just in time for the morning rush." He groaned at the line that was almost out the front doors.

Instead of waiting in line, she took his hand and moved through the crowd until they sat at an empty booth along the back wall.

"I texted Jessie. She's got our back." She smiled and nodded towards the front counter. "It pays to have friends in the right places."

When Jessie set two cups of coffee and a large plate of cinnamon rolls in front of them, he groaned with happiness.

"Marry me." He took Jessie's hand and lifted it to his lips. "The woman of my dreams." He turned to Xtina. "Well, both of you are." He winked at her.

"Sorry, can't stay to enjoy the irony of my best friend's boyfriend proposing to me…" Jessie chuckled and rushed off.

Xtina had taken a swallow of coffee and almost choked on it.

"What? Did you find it odd that she called you her best friend or that she thinks I'm your boyfriend?" He smiled big as he picked up his cup of coffee and took a large drink.

"No." She coughed a few times, then took another drink of her coffee. "I mean, of course we're best friends." Her eyes traveled everywhere but to his. Reaching over, he took her hand in his, stopping her from reaching for a cinnamon roll.

"I rather like that people think of us as going out," he said, and her eyes finally settled on his. "Going steady."

"I…" She shrugged. "That's not a term most people use." She chuckled and rolled her eyes. "I mean, normally…" She groaned and reached for her coffee with her free hand.

He chuckled. "How about we leave it at that for now." He released her hand. "Now, the question at hand is… Who gets the big roll and who gets the smaller one?"

She laughed and, in the end, he enjoyed the big cinnamon roll and almost half of hers since she said she couldn't finish it.

By the time the plates were empty and the coffee was gone, Jacob had walked in.

Michael saw Xtina's eyes sober up and her smile waver.

"No matter what happens, have an open mind," she said under her breath before Jacob stopped at

155

their table.

"Mind if I join you?" he asked, then he slid in next to Xtina when they both nodded.

"How'd everything go?" Mike asked, his eyes traveling between Xtina and Jacob. He wasn't sure why she'd wanted to have coffee with the man, but he was open-minded enough to see how things would unfold.

"Fine. I'm pretty sure you both will be getting calls from the local paper any minute." He groaned. "We've been flooded with calls after someone leaked information about you."

Mike felt his entire body tense. "How far has it reached?"

"So far, only the local paper." He nodded to Jessie, who put up a finger to tell him just a moment. "But I'm sure that after the local guys run something, others will follow."

Jessie made her way over to the table with a cup and a plate with a blueberry bagel and cream cheese on it.

"Hey." She glanced over at Jacob, then sat down next to Mike with her own cup of coffee. "So," she turned to Xtina. "I heard you had quite the exciting night." She leaned in as Xtina quickly relayed what had happened.

"So, that's where we're at." Xtina finished the story and leaned back in the booth as Jacob finished off his bagel. "Now we're tired and ready for some quiet."

"I bet. I'm sorry I wasn't there," Jess said as her phone beeped on the table. Rolling her eyes, she slowly got up. "Break time is over. How about I come out this evening with a bottle of wine?"

"Make it margaritas and I'll heat up my mom's chicken enchiladas that I found in the back of the freezer yesterday."

"Sounds perfect." She waved as she disappeared behind the counter again.

"I didn't know you and Jessica were friends," Jacob said, turning slightly towards Xtina.

"We went to school together," she said absently. He could tell that she was at the end of her energy.

"Chrissy?" Jacob turned and squinted his eyes more at her. "Hell, I guess I was too busy interviewing Laura Schmitt that I didn't think to check over your file."

"I always hated it when you called me that." She groaned.

"You two know each other?" Mike asked, stating the obvious, but hey, he'd just gone an entire night without sleep.

"We did grow up here in Hidden Creek." Jacob's smile brightened slightly. "Course, we were on opposite sides of the field. So to speak." He relaxed back. "And I was two years ahead in class."

"I didn't recognize you at first. Of course a lot has changed since I saw you last." She bit her bottom lip.

"Are you going to tell me why you invited me out for coffee?" he finally said after a moment of silence. "I'm not dying of cancer, am I?"

Xtina looked as if she'd been punched in the gut. "Oh, god no. Is that what you thought?" Her eyes traveled between them as a shocked look crossed her eyes. "As far as I know, you're healthy and fit." She relaxed a little when Jacob chuckled.

"That's good to know," he murmured. "So, why then?"

Her eyes moved to his, then she shifted in her seat. "I wanted to talk to you about your family."

"Okay?" He drew the word out. "My dad? My mom? They're both okay?"

"Yes, I'm sorry. Everyone is fine. I meant, your birth family."

Mike saw the man tense. "I know enough about them; they didn't want me. Period."

"No, you don't." Xtina glanced at him. "Otherwise, you would know that you're sitting across the table from your brother."

"What the hell?" Michael's voice traveled throughout the semi-crowded coffee shop.

"What kind of joke is this?" Jacob added at the same time.

158

"It's no joke." Xtina reached for Michael's hand, only to have him jerk it away.

"Is this what you saw? That I'm his brother?" he asked.

She nodded slightly when both men turned towards her. "Your parents"—she glanced towards Michael— "were young. I'm guessing sixteen, seventeen when they had Jacob. Back then, at least in Hidden Creek, it was unheard of to have a child at such an age."

"They would have told us," Michael said under his breath.

"You're the same," she added. "I can't read much from you." She turned to Jacob. "And you know how to block me."

"Me?" He balked. "How would I know how to do that?"

She shrugged. "Maybe it's your own kind of power?"

He snorted. "Right."

"We all have different kinds of powers. Michael has an ability to find hidden things, to see the truth." Her eyes met his and he felt as if the way he'd felt his entire life had finally been confirmed. "That and he can block my scans. Just like you can, but I did see enough." She turned to Jacob and for a split second, Michael felt a surge of jealousy.

They were sitting close, on the same side of the

booth. He hadn't thought anything of it until now, seeing them so close together. His eyes traveled over the man she was claiming was his brother.

Sure, they had the same hair coloring, the same skin tone, but that was as far as the similarities went. Jacob had almost an entire foot on him, his nose was different, his eyes were more... he lost his train of thought. More like his father's. Even the man's chin was a fit with his dad's.

He'd always joked with his brother Ethan that they'd gotten the short end of the straw by looking so much like their mother.

Jacob was almost a spitting image of Michael's father. Without listening any more to Xtina, he knew she was right. Michael was sitting across the table from a brother he'd never known existed.

***

Xtina pushed Jacob out of the booth quickly so she could catch up with Michael as he stormed out of the coffee shop.

"I'll..." She glanced over her shoulder at Jacob.

"Yeah, later," he said, frowning down into his empty coffee mug.

She caught up with Michael less than a block away.

"I have to go," he said, still walking towards the main road.

"Don't." She took his arm and pulled him to a

stop. "Let me drive you home."

"No, it's only two miles. I could use the fresh air." He jerked his hand away, but before storming off, he turned towards her. "You could have told me." His eyes looked tired and she knew that he was right.

"Michael, I did what I was supposed to. You both deserved to know, together."

His eyes narrowed, then he nodded and turned away.

"Come over for dinner," she called after him. "We can talk some more."

He continued to walk down the busy street without even glancing back at her.

"He'll be okay," Jacob said right behind her, causing her to jump slightly.

Normally she would have sensed the presence behind her, but just like with Michael, Jacob was a hidden spot to her.

"Yes, how about you?" She turned and looked into his eyes.

"For years I've wondered if I had a family out there. Brothers or sisters. I've gone my entire life wondering." He nodded to where Michael was disappearing around the bend of the road. "He's never wondered. Never imagined that he would have a loose end out there somewhere."

Her hand settled on his arm. "You're not a loose

end. You're family."

His eyes met hers. "And we both know how screwed up family can be."

"Yes, I remember." Her eyes moved to their joined skin as she remembered how strict his adopted father was. "Has he gotten any better with age?"

"Worse." His tone told her that he wanted to drop the subject. "Looks like I have an excuse to finally dig into my adoption papers."

She turned to him with a questioning look.

"I want to know what kind of screwed-up family I'm now part of." He turned to go. "Chrissy…" She glared at him. "Xtina, thanks."

She smiled. "Anytime. If you need anything…"

He nodded, then turned to walk towards his car.

Since she was now bursting with energy, she decided to swing by the grocery store and pick up a few things she might need for dinner.

She walked the block to the grocery store, pulled out a cart, and started pulling items together for a salad. Her mind was so preoccupied with Michael that she bumped solidly into a thin blonde woman.

"Sorry," she murmured, catching herself just before she reached out to steady the woman.

"Oh." The blonde turned towards her. When her crystal blue eyes met Xtina's, a blinding light seared her mind, just before everything went blank.

She woke in her own living room, with Jessie hovering over her.

"Not again." She groaned. "Now what?"

"You did an impressive face dive into the salad section at Smelly Kelly's," a male voice said from a few feet away.

The entire town had called the small grocery store that since a particularly bad incident when she was back in high school when a large rat had crawled into the air conditioning unit and died. The place had been closed down for a week to air out.

Her head was spinning, and she decided not to turn her head to see who was talking just yet.

"Why can't this end?" she groaned.

"She's fine now, you can go," Jessie said in a strict voice. She listened to her front door open and close, then she looked into Jessie's eyes.

"I'm sorry to bring him here," her friend murmured. "But I didn't know where Michael had gone to and he wasn't answering his phone."

"He's mad at me." She moved slightly, causing the entire room to spin once more. "I feel like I was hit by a truck." She gripped her head.

"No, just the edge of the salad bar at Kelly's."

"Who was that?" With her eyes closed, she nodded slightly towards the front door.

She looked up at Jess, who was looking nervously at her and biting her bottom lip.

"Like I said, I'm sorry to bring him here, but he is the one who brought you to me. And he was being so nice about it too. He didn't even call an ambulance or anything."

"Jessica." She used her friend's full name, one that she knew she hated.

"Fine, it was Joe." This time it was Xtina who groaned.

"Great." She felt a shiver race through her body. "At least tell me he didn't carry…" She didn't get any further when she heard Jessie sniffle.

"Sorry. I didn't know what else to do. They were going to call the ambulance. Do you remember the last time you woke up in a hospital after—"?

"Yes, thank you." She reached over and took her friend's hand. She was too tired to brace for the images, and instead, allowed them to lull her back to sleep.

When she woke again, it was to pans being dropped in the kitchen.

"Sorry!" Jessie called out.

Xtina sat up slowly. Her entire body was stiff and she took a moment to roll her shoulders before standing up.

Glancing at the clock, she gauged she'd had about six hours of sleep. Which meant Jessie was probably trying to heat up dinner. She felt grimy and gross and decided a quick shower was in order. Climbing the stairs slowly, she took her time under the hot spray, letting the heat relax every muscle that was screaming at her for sleeping on the uncomfortable sofa. When she was done, she pulled on a pair of black yoga pants and a large Colorado Avalanche sweatshirt and made her way down to help Jess out with dinner.

"I'm sorry I didn't get salad—" she started to say as she walked into the kitchen and saw a full salad laid out on the table. "Never mind." She sat down at the countertop, then smiled when Jessie pushed a large margarita towards her.

"Did you get enough sleep?" Jessie asked, turning back towards the stove.

"Enough for now. Have you been here all day?"

"Yes and no. I did make a quick run to the store to get the salad and these." She held up her glass so Xtina could clink them together. "To catching killers and passing out in the fresh food section." Jessie's smile grew.

"Bite me." She chuckled, then took a long drink of the cool liquid. "Mmm. Perfect." She turned to her friend. "You know, after everything that's happened in the last few days, I'm beginning to think that your talent is seeing what people want. Not only that, but delivering it, too."

Jessie smiled. "You're on to me." She wiggled her eyebrows. "But I promise to only use my super powers for good and not evil." She raised her arm above her head and then spun around towards the stove. "My empath senses are tingling, telling me you want... chicken enchiladas."

Xtina laughed. "And they would be spot on."

They hung out in the kitchen eating chicken enchiladas and drinking a whole pitcher of margaritas. Then they took a fresh pitcher of drinks onto the front porch and sat out on the swing as Xtina filled Jessie in on Michael and Jacob.

"You did the right thing," Jess said after she'd filled her in all the way.

"No, he's right. I should have told him first." She closed her eyes and felt the guilt settle in. Her eyes had darted towards his place more than a dozen times since they'd gone out onto the porch.

"You can't second-guess your decisions. If you feel strongly about it, go... talk to him. But you did what you felt you had to do."

She glanced once more towards his place. The lights were off, but she could see the faint glow of a computer screen in the area he had set up as an office.

"Will you be okay here?" She nodded towards the house.

"Sure, I'll crash on your sofa for a while, maybe watch a movie on your new TV. Which is awesome, by the way." She winked. "Now I want to save up my money and buy a new one."

"Okay, but I'm taking this." She snagged the pitcher and carried it with her across the yard.

"Make sure to use protection," Jess called after her.

"Shut up!" she called back, hearing Jessie giggle in her wake.

Chapter Eleven

$\mathcal{S}$ince Mike had walked back into his house, he'd been punching away on his computer keyboard learning everything he could about Jacob St. Clair. The man was pretty much an open book.

He seemed to have nothing to hide. It probably shouldn't be a surprise—he'd been raised in Hidden Creek, one of the smallest, friendliest, easygoing towns in the south.

Who living here would have anything major to hide? It wasn't as if murders like the one that had happened last night were the norm around here. If it really was murder, it would be their first homicide in almost twenty years.

There were plenty of missing persons,

accidents, and other incidental arrests, but nothing as big as murdering a husband so someone could have an affair.

The last time that had happened—he felt his body shiver with the memory—a schoolteacher had been sent over the edge and a housewife to the end of a lake.

From what he could tell, Jacob had been adopted in Atlanta and brought to Hidden Creek less than a week after his birth. Since his birth records were closed, he couldn't officially confirm that they had the same parents. Nor did he feel like picking up his phone and confronting them. At least not until he'd gotten some sleep.

He glanced over at the sofa and decided a quick nap would do him some good. Then he could tackle this fresh and see if there was anything he'd missed.

He flung himself onto the sofa and was out the second his head hit the cushions.

His mind wandered in sleep. Images came and went, but the only steady thought was of Xtina. Her green eyes pulled him into a realm where magic was the norm.

People floated above the ground, fairies buzzed around the grassy forest, bright green leaves softly floated in the breeze, and the trees swayed gently in the wind.

He was walking with her, hand in hand, up a

hill covered with small yellow and pink flowers.

One minute they were smiling and gazing into one another's eyes, and then the next, a large cloud floated over their heads. The entire atmosphere changed and suddenly Xtina dropped his hand and started running away from him. He took off after her, but his feet felt like they were stuck in mud. Each step took so much energy he was quickly losing ground.

He called out for her, but his voice didn't seem to work. When she made it to the top of a small hill, she stopped. A bright light was pulsing from beyond the trees, almost blinding him.

Then a bright blue flash caused Xtina to disappear completely and he woke with a start, his scream still deep in his lungs.

He'd jerked himself into a sitting position. Running his hands over his face, he reached down for his iPad when there was a knock at his door.

Setting his iPad on the kitchen table, he walked to the door while thinking about starting a fire in the fireplace, since the new flooring he'd put down was cold on his bare feet.

When he opened his door, he forgot about his cold feet. Xtina stood leaning against his doorframe, a margarita in one hand and what he could only presume was a full pitcher of the stuff in the other hand.

He hadn't been too upset with her about her keeping the information to herself about Jacob.

Still, he'd needed some space after she'd dropped the news on them in the coffee shop. The walk had cleared away all the hurt and anger, enough that once he'd gotten home, he'd had enough clarity to start doing research.

"Hey." She smiled up at him and he could tell that she was a little intoxicated.

"Hey." He leaned against the doorjamb much like her. "Looks like your dinner with Jessie turned out good."

She giggled. "I passed out."

He reached for her hand. "When?" He took her shoulders and led her to the sofa, making sure to take the drinks from her and set them on the coffee table that had just been delivered yesterday.

Looking down at her, he noticed that she now had a frown on her face. "When you left me."

"At the coffee shop?" She shook her head. "Then when?"

"Smelly Kelly's. The grocery store. I went to get salad." She hiccupped, then reached for her drink. "Then I…" She frowned again. "I passed out."

He took her drink from her hand again and set it down. "Maybe you'd better start from the beginning." He sat next to her and took her hands in his.

"You were mad, and…"

"I wasn't mad," he interrupted.

She glared at him. "Yes you were. You walked away."

"Doesn't mean I was mad." He rubbed his thumb over the back of her hand and enjoyed the shiver he felt from her because of it.

"You walked away," she said again, her eyes coming back to his. "So, I decided to go to the store for salad for tonight. I was just picking out the tomatoes or maybe it was cucumbers." She tilted her head slightly. "When I think I bumped into someone. I guess the images were too much for me to handle on so little sleep." She shrugged. "I woke up on my sofa."

"How did you get home?"

"Jess." Her eyes moved back to her drink. "Do you want any of this?" She took another sip.

"Later." He waited until she turned back to him. "I'm sorry. I shouldn't have left."

He watched her shoulders rise and fall. "It's okay. I should have told you about Jacob... before, when I found out."

"No, you did what you felt was right. I shouldn't have left you alone especially after everything you went through last night."

He once again set her drink down, chuckling this time when she made a face at him. He tugged on her shoulders until she fell against his chest. Then his fingers dug into her hair as he gently forced her to look up at him.

"I wasn't mad, I'm not mad at you. I just needed some time. I shouldn't have left you alone." He leaned his forehead against hers. She wrapped her arms around his body and all the desires from the past weeks surfaced.

He'd tried to hold back all his feelings, everything he'd been wanting to do to her, with her. But when her fingers reached up under his shirt and touched his bare skin, he knew there was no holding back the flood any longer. His fingers tightened in her hair, and he tilted her head back.

"Look at me." It came out almost as a growl. When her green eyes met his, he could tell that she wasn't too drunk to know what she was doing. "Tell me to stop. Tell me to go to hell, tell me anything."

"No." She shook her head slightly and he relaxed his fingers enough that he didn't accidently yank her hair. "I can't. I've wanted this too much." Her eyes stayed locked with his as she leaned over and brushed her lips against his, softly.

It was the softness that made his entire body relax. He'd been wound up tight, ready to spring, but now, he all he wanted to give her was softness.

In one quick swoop, he laid her down on the sofa and had her tucked underneath his body, their lips never leaving one another's. His fingers left her soft hair, traveling slowly down the column of her neck, feeling each of her heartbeats with his fingertips. He raced over the thickness of her sweatshirt until he reached the hem of the oversized material, then pushed it gently up and over her shoulders in one quick motion.

When he leaned back to enjoy the view, he realized she was completely bare underneath the sweatshirt. His eyes slowly traveled over her exposed skin as a slow smile crept onto his lips.

"So beautiful," he said as her eyes met his. She was biting her bottom lip in worry.

Gently, he ran a fingertip up her body and watched her green eyes turn brighter with desire. When he leaned down to once more run his mouth over her skin, she moaned. Her entire body shivered as his fingers brushed gently up her exposed skin. Her back arched when he ran his mouth over the same trail.

When her fingers dug into his hair, he groaned against her skin and enjoyed the taste of her soft skin against his lips as his fingers trailed over the leggings she was wearing. The tight material hugged her curves, exposing every soft spot he wanted to explore.

He heard her begging him, moaning whenever his lips found a spot that she enjoyed. He took his time exploring every soft inch of her, until he cupped her gently with his hands and her shoulders once more jerked from the cushions.

"Michael." She said his name over and over as

she continued to writhe underneath him. When he tugged her leggings down those long legs of hers, he felt her tense momentarily. And upon seeing her completely exposed skin, he knew why she'd hesitated. As with above, she was completely bare underneath.

"Do you normally go without panties and a bra?" he asked, his eyes glued to her exposed skin.

"Only when I plan on seducing my neighbor," she said in a breathless tone.

"It's working." He finished pulling the leggings down her long legs and then ran his hands smoothly up and down them.

Then in one quick motion, he lifted her from the sofa and carried her back into his bedroom. When he laid her down gently on the bed, he took another moment to just enjoy the view. He was thankful that he'd gotten a box of condoms at the store a few weeks back.

"Michael, don't make me wait." Xtina held up her hands towards him.

***

She'd never felt so right about something in her entire life. Her feelings for Michael had been growing since the first time she'd laid eyes on him.

Her desires had only grown when she'd discovered that she couldn't read him. She'd always had to block or be careful when choosing to be close to someone. She forced her mind to not wander too far into her past. Instead, she focused on Michael's touch. His fingers running up and down her sides, his lips on her neck, trailing heated kisses down her shoulders until his mouth covered first one breast, then another.

A gasp escaped her as her back arched up with excitement. She'd never experienced something so primitive as the feeling of his teeth nipping at her skin. His fingers traveled down her flat stomach until he once more cupped her. Only this time, he rubbed a finger across her, sending a million stars to explode behind her eyelids.

She couldn't stop the half-scream that escaped her lips when his finger dipped slowly into her. She heard his own groan of desire as his mouth left her breast to travel down the plane of her stomach until it settled over the spot his fingers had just been.

"Michael," she cried out when he started lapping at her skin, his fingers still moving around his mouth.

"You're so sweet," he said between heavy breaths. "So perfect." He groaned as her nails dug into his shoulders, trying to hold him closer to her.

"I need…" She felt her chest tighten. "I…" She cried out when her entire body convulsed for him.

She'd never experienced anything like the power that emanated from him as he crawled up her body and settled over her. She felt him reach for something on his nightstand, but kept her eyes

176

closed and just enjoyed the feeling of his skin against hers.

She didn't remember him removing his shirt, but enjoyed the feeling of that sexy chest rubbing up against her own heated skin. Her fingers ran over his shoulders, enjoying the cord of muscles that played over his back.

He shifted again and she could tell he was removing his jeans.

"This I have to see." She leaned her head up slightly and smiled when his eyes met hers. "What? You think you're the only one who can enjoy tonight?" She chuckled when he frowned up at her.

"No, of course not." He tossed his jeans across the room, then she watched him smoothly slide on a condom. "Well?" he said once the task was done. "How do I rate?" His smile was back when he moved closer to her.

"Easily a ten." She reached for him, but he moved back and raised his eyebrows as he laughed.

"You're only saying that because you want to sleep with me," he joked.

"And wouldn't you rate me a ten right now too?" She waited as his eyes ran slowly over her.

"Now, tomorrow, the next day." His eyes met hers. "A year from now." His smile slowly fell from his lips. "Actually, I can't foresee any time in

177

our future that I won't think that."

She felt her heart skip and her throat go completely dry. "Michael."

He shook his head. "Later," he said softly, then moved to cover her. "Now, let's enjoy what we have." He came back down and kissed her. She poured everything she was feeling into the kiss as her arms and legs wrapped around his body.

When he arched his back, she opened for him and felt the pure enjoyment of him sliding slowly into her. She couldn't stop her legs from tightening further around his hips.

Their mouths met once more and she cried out with pure joy with every thrust. Her nails dug into his skin as she felt herself once more building and knew that she wanted to wait for him this time.

"Please," she cried out as their speeds quickened. "Michael, I can't..." She shook her head, her lips brushing the spot next to his ear. "I won't go without you," she said softly into his ear.

"You first," he groaned. "I want to see your eyes turn." His eyes jerked up as their eyes met. "Now." He groaned as his hips moved over her. "It has to be..."

"Now!" she screamed. Their eyes locked as she felt her entire body spasm along with his.

**

She must have slept for a few minutes because when she woke, their skin had cooled down and she actually felt herself shiver in the cool night air.

"Damn," he cursed. "I meant to start a fire tonight." She felt him shift just before a thick blanket settled over her body.

"Don't go." She reached for him, stopping him from leaving the bed.

"It won't take more than a moment. Would you like some water?" His eyes softened as they ran over her face.

She knew she probably looked a mess. Her hair had been still a little damp from her shower when she'd knocked on his door. Now, it probably looked like a rat's nest. She hadn't put on any makeup before coming over, which was one more reason she wanted the room to remain as dark as possible.

She tested herself and realized that she could use some water.

"Yes," she finally answered him, her mind racing to how she could escape into his bathroom and at least comb through her hair.

"If you need anything…" He brushed a finger down her cheek. "Let me know."

"I'm fine." She swallowed. "Just water."

He nodded, then leaned down and pulled on his jeans. He stopped at the door, cursed under his breath, then walked over to his closet and pulled on a pair of socks. "Damn wood floor is freezing. I can't wait until under the house is sealed up," he complained as he walked out of the room.

She waited until he was out of sight before she darted for the bathroom. When she closed the door behind her, she realized how true his words were. Her feet were freezing. She closed her eyes as she flipped on the light in his bathroom.

She almost squealed when she realized that his window had no covering and she was standing in the bright room bare naked.

Grabbing a towel from his rack, she quickly tied it around her body and walked over to shut his blinds. Not that there were any neighbors close… she laughed when she realized she was actually his closest neighbor.

She spent enough time brushing through her hair and washing her face that when she walked back into the bedroom, her feet were almost numb with the cold.

"You must be freezing," he said from the end of the bed. "Come climb in." He patted the spot next to him on the bed. "I made us some hot chocolate and grabbed this…" He held up a bag of popcorn. "I figured we can talk and have a snack."

She rushed across the room and jumped in the bed, making sure to tuck her feet under herself to warm them up quickly.

"Here." He turned her around, moving his warm legs against her feet. "My god!" he exclaimed when her cold feet touched his skin. "You're freezing. That's it, I'm sealing under the house tomorrow and having them install the HVAC system as soon as possible."

Her teeth stopped shivering when the hot liquid slid down her throat. "Mmm." She groaned with pleasure. "It's good." She rested back against his chest. He'd pulled on a T-shirt and she silently wished for something other than a large towel to wear.

"Here, have some." He held open the bag of popcorn. It was still warm from the microwave and the smell caused her stomach to growl.

"I don't know why I'm so hungry. We finished off the entire pan of chicken enchiladas earlier."

This time it was his stomach that growled. He chuckled. "Shhh, don't say it too loud. I only had a cold turkey sandwich earlier."

"I did invite you over for dinner." She glanced up at him and grabbed another handful of popcorn. "Remember?"

He nodded. "I was busy doing some research."

"On?" she asked, taking another sip of hot chocolate.

"My brother." His tone flattened.

Her eyes met his again. "I'm sorry."

He shook his head. "Don't be." He shifted and set his own mug of hot liquid down on the nightstand. "I've done everything I can, except call

181

my parents to confirm."

"And?" She waited.

"From everything I can tell, it could be true. My parents were raised in Hidden Creek. Actually, it's one of the reasons I chose to move here. That and the fact that it has the least crime in the entire state."

She nodded and finished off her hot chocolate. "What did you find?"

"Well, I know from what my parents have told me that the summer of their junior year, they both went to camp. My mother told me how she had been so sick that summer that she'd actually missed the first month of her senior year."

"Do you think…" she started, only to have him nod in agreement.

"I checked around. The only camp that was running back then was Holly Grove. The summer of their junior year, Holly Grove had been closed due to repairs. They didn't open back up for almost two years, after it had changed ownership."

"I'm sorry," she added again.

His arm moved around her and he pulled her close.

"What are you going to do now?" she asked, enjoying the feeling of his chest rising and falling underneath her head.

"I guess I'll have to call them in the morning."

He scooted down further until they were laying down. "I'm sorry about leaving you alone today." She started to shake her head, but he stopped her. "I shouldn't have left you alone." His hand brushed through her hair, touching her neck underneath, causing goose bumps to rise all over.

"Michael." She sighed and drifted into sleep.

Chapter Twelve

Once more, his night was shattered when he felt the building of energy in his room. After a year of it, he was becoming accustomed to the figure appearing at the foot of his bed. What he wasn't prepared for this time was the warm soft body that was tangled with his own.

"Xtina," he said softly, "our visitor is here." He couldn't believe how normal his tone was.

"Hmm, she'll go away," she murmured.

He glanced at his clock and frowned. "It's almost two." He frowned and looked at the figure. "She never stays that late."

Xtina's eyes opened slightly and she sat up. "What is it?" she said. Only afterwards did he realize she wasn't asking him.

The figure moved towards the window, then he watched in amazement as her hand rose and she actually pointed out it. Her eyes moved back to Xtina's, then his.

"Go," she mouthed. "Now."

Shivers spiked all over his body.

"What?" he asked when Xtina started getting up from the bed. His hand reached for hers. "You can't be serious?"

She turned and looked at him as the figure started to disappear. Her eyebrows were arched up. "She wants us to go somewhere."

"At two in the morning?" he growled out.

She nodded slightly. "I've learned not to question it too much. Besides, tell me you can fall back asleep after that." She motioned to the empty spot at his window.

He groaned. "Fine, but let's put on some clothes first." His eyes moved to her exposed skin.

"Well, duh." She smiled. "Go grab my clothes from the…" She stopped when he held them up. "Thanks." She leaned over and kissed him quickly. "Do you have a jacket?" she said once she was dressed. "I kind of left my house without one."

"Yeah, I've got a couple flashlights too." He pulled out his winter coat from the closet and handed it to her. "It's probably big, but then…" He tugged on the Colorado sweatshirt and she got the hint.

"It wasn't another man's. I just bought it big so I could…" She shook her head. "Never mind." She slid on the jacket and took the flashlight from his hands. "Let's go."

"Where?" he asked once they were outside. "She pointed that way," he said towards her house, but then turned and shrugged. "Does she want you to go home?"

"No." She shook her head. "Jessie's there." Then worry crossed her eyes and she took off towards the house quickly.

"Xtina," he called after her, catching up with her before the porch. "What's wrong? You don't think…" He dropped off when she stopped at the front door, their breaths bursting from them in quick puffs of smoke.

"Please, oh please…" She closed her eyes and then opened the door slowly.

The room was dark and he reached over and flipped the beam of light into the room. There was a small figure on the sofa, curled up tight under a thick blanket.

"She's okay," Xtina said, then turned back towards the doorway. She jumped back quickly and gasped. He turned, ready to spring into action, when he noticed the figure standing on her porch.

"Go," she mouthed again. This time she pointed

slightly to the left. "Now."

Xtina glanced back quickly to her sleeping friend. "Scared me," she said as she shut her front door.

"Yeah." He took her hand and walked towards the figure that was floating off towards the forest. "Now we just need to follow a ghost…."

"Not a ghost," she supplied, causing him to smile.

"Right. Now we just need to follow that"—he nodded towards the figure— "into the dark woods, in the middle of the night armed with only flashlights and our wits." He chuckled. "For some reason every eighties horror movie is playing in my mind right now."

She chuckled. "Stop it. I'm sure she just wants to show us something."

"Right, like the ghost in Poltergeist…. or the one in the Shining where the girls want Danny to play." He shivered visibly.

She slapped at his arm playfully. "Now you've got me freaked out."

"That's great. Coming from the girl who vanquished her first ghost at the tender age of…."

They followed slowly along. He took her arm a few times to help her over a fallen tree branch.

"How much farther do you think?" he asked, feeling like a child.

"I don't know. When I was a kid, I used to explore these woods. At least when I could escape. I spent countless hours out here, but..." She shook her head. "I've never been this far in."

"Maybe we should go back?" He glanced over his shoulder then down at his watch and saw that they had been gone almost an hour.

"No, let's keep going." She took his hand. They walked for another ten minutes until they finally came to a big clearing.

"This is the edge of the Miller's Farm." She stopped and nodded towards a long barbed-wire fence across the field. "I'm not sure who this field belongs to, but that"—she pointed to an old barn—"is Bob Miller's dairy farm."

The smell had hit him a while ago and he knew there were cattle around somewhere. "She stopped moving." He nodded to the figure. She stood in the middle of the field, her misty form hovering above the grain that was gently blowing in the night wind.

"Let's go see." Xtina took his hand.

"Has she ever done this before?" he asked as they moved closer.

"No. Then again, she's never tried to say anything before either." The figure turned towards them, then drifted into nothingness.

"Guess this is where she wants..." he started to say, then felt something solid under his foot. He

188

moved his flashlight to the ground, then wrapped his arms around Xtina quickly to stop her from moving forward.

"What?" she gasped, then glanced down to where his flashlight beam hit.

There, in the middle of a grain field, was a gaping hole leading down into blackness.

***

Xtina squeezed Michael's hand harder. "What is it?"

"Looks like an old missile silo. They were built all over the States during the Cold War." He took a giant step back, making sure to take her with him. "We'll have to come back out here when it's daylight."

"Why did she have us come now?" She took out her flashlight and inched forward. "There must be..." She gasped when the beam hit something white and covered in fur. "There." She pointed. "What is that?"

She waited as he moved slowly around and got a better look. "Looks like a dog," he said. "I don't think it's moving. It must have—" A small cry echoed from the massive hole. "Damn," he said, moving closer. "Looks like I'm going in."

"You can't." She walked around to him.

"There's a ladder here." He pointed his beam to the other side. "If you'll shine the light, I can see if

189

the rungs will hold up."

"This is crazy. You can't risk your life for—"

He turned to her, stopping her words. She took a deep breath. "But you're going to anyway. Aren't you?"

He smiled. "Shine the light here." He moved her hand to where she could clearly see the metal rungs. They looked strong enough. Actually, the entire thing looked like it had been covered up until recently. There wasn't even any rust that she could see.

She held her breath as he took his time, one rung at a time.

"They're pretty stable," he called up to her once he reached the bottom. "Easy," he said to the dog, who was now growling softly. "It looks like a border collie," he called up. "Its leg is injured, but everything else looks good." She heard him speaking softly to the animal.

Silently she wished she'd remembered to grab her cell phone at her place.

Why would the entity worry about an injured dog? She'd never experienced anyone from beyond concerned about living creatures. Even thought she'd always known this particular entity wasn't a ghost, she had always assumed that it still abided by rules.

One had been that she'd always remained at the old McCullen place. Two, that it couldn't talk or

190

communicate, and three, that it didn't interact with living things. All three of which had been proven incorrect in the past few days.

"You okay?" she called down after too many moments went by filled with silence.

"I'm trying to use my coat as a sling so I can carry it up." He cursed. "Okay, I think we're ready," he finally said. "I'll need lots of light. Think you can hold my flashlight too?"

She bent down and flipped on his light, making sure to have the beams hit each rung as he climbed slowly up.

When he made it to the top, she released the breath she'd been holding. He sat in the dirt, breathing hard, covered in a light sheen of sweat.

"I bet this isn't how you planned to spend our first morning together." He chuckled, then nodded towards the first rays of sunlight rising over the field.

She ran a hand over the dog's soft coat. "No, but I bet she didn't plan on spending her night stuck in a dark hole waiting for two people and a ghost to save her."

"Ghost?" he asked.

"Whatever. I'm tired of fighting it. She's not like anything I've ever experienced." Her eyes met his. "Why would she care about a dog?"

His eyes moved back to the hole. "I don't think

191

she did." Her eyes followed his and she felt a shiver when she noticed the glimmer of light coming from the bottom.

"Later," he said. "This time I'm insisting." He said it loudly enough for both her and the entity to hear. They both watched as the light grew dark. "I've got her." He lifted the dog gently into his arms. "Later we're going to have a talk about how you know it's a she." His eyes moved to hers. "But for now, lead the way back, I'll follow."

She tucked his flashlight into the coat pocket and started back the way they came. Instead of going all the way to his place, she stopped at her back door.

"I've got a first aid kit." She opened the back door. "Upstairs." She put her finger over her mouth to keep him quiet, but when they walked into the kitchen, Jessie was standing at the stove, a hot cup of coffee in her hand and a spatula swirling around in one of her mother's cast iron pans.

"Morning…" she said, then turned and gasped when she saw them. "What happened?" She set the spatula down and rushed towards them. "Oh, you poor thing. Was it hit?"

"No, it fell," Xtina supplied as Michael laid it gently down on the rug.

"I'll get the kit and some old blankets." She quickly disappeared up the stairs. When she came back down, Jessie was piling a big scoop of eggs and bacon onto plates.

"I figured you'd be hungry after your trek." She set the food down.

Xtina looked to Michael. "Don't ask me how she knew."

"Well, it wasn't as if you two were stealth leaving here. I saw you head into the woods and figured you'd gone for some crazy walk." She shrugged and then sat down. "So, are you going to fill me in?"

"Later." She handed Michael the kit and towels. "How's she doing?"

"Much better. Her leg doesn't look broken, and she's actually moving it around. I think she's just in shock and cold."

Xtina ran a hand over the dog once more. "And pregnant," she added with a smile.

"Okay, totally freaked out right now." He glanced towards Jessie.

"Don't look at me. She's always been an animal whisperer." She rolled her eyes. "She's the one that told me my cat, Mr. Rogers, hated his name and preferred Limp Bizkit instead."

Michael chuckled. "You're making that up."

Jessie motioned to Xtina, who just nodded.

"He'd seen them on TV once and liked the music."

Michael laughed, fully, causing her to laugh

193

too. Soon the entire room was full of laughter. Xtina laid her hand on the dog again and smiled. "She likes the sound of our laughter. She'll sleep for a while, if she can have some of the bacon." She nodded to Jessie, who handed over two slices. "Here, you give it to her. She's smitten with you." Xtina winked at Michael, then chuckled when she saw his cheeks heat.

They sat around her kitchen table and ate Jessie's breakfast as the sun rose and the injured dog slept. When Jessie disappeared upstairs to shower, they talked about their plans to return to the silo later that day and do some serious exploring.

Both of them agreed that at least a shower and a few more hours of sleep were in order before they made the trek again.

"We've got to plan this out better. Bigger flash lights, emergency supplies," he was saying when Jessie appeared again, freshly showered.

"Going camping?" she asked, swallowing the last of her coffee.

"Um, more like exploring," Xtina said. "We found an old missile silo."

"Cool, is it the one near the Miller's?"

Xtina and Michael turned to her.

"What?" She shrugged and stuffed the last piece of bacon into her mouth. "My folks used to go out there when they were kids. Actually, a lot of people did." She turned to Xtina. "Even your parents."

"How do you know?" she asked.

"I saw a picture of them…"—she flung her purse over her shoulder— "in my mom's high school year book." She started towards the door.

"Can you bring it by later tonight?" Xtina asked.

"Sure, I work a full shift today, so I won't be by until after dinner."

"Okay." She watched her friend go and wondered why Jessie had never mentioned seeing the picture of her parents before.

Michael's hand reached out and touched hers. "While she's still asleep and we have the house to ourselves, why don't we head up and shower. I'm filthy and smell like wet dog." He nodded to the stairs and she felt her heart skip. He smiled.

"Sure." She took her plate to the sink.

"I'm going to run home and get a few things, a change of clothes. I'll be right back." He walked to the front and disappeared.

Moving over to the sleeping dog, she pushed her hands through the dog's soft fur. It was dry now and she thought about giving it a bath later that evening so she didn't smell, something even the dog agreed with, apparently.

"Rose." Xtina smiled. "What a perfect name,"

she said softly. It was one of the dog's favorite smells.

She'd always loved animals. Unfortunately, after her parents had found out that she could sense them, they had never allowed any in their house.

Glancing around, she raised her chin. This was her house now.

Standing up, she put her hands on her hips and looked around. She hadn't changed much since moving in. She had a coffee maker, a new microwave, a TV, and a few other things, but nothing major.

The walls were still that bright yellow she'd always hated growing up. The floors were old cracked tile that was too cold in the winters and too hard for her liking. Then there were the rooms upstairs. She was still sleeping in the small room she'd had as a child while her parents' large master bedroom sat empty.

She hadn't even gone in their room yet, let alone thought about moving in. Their bathroom was huge, much like their bedroom, yet she'd crammed herself into the small guest bathroom she'd shared with her grandmother when she'd lived there.

Well, it was time she changed all that. She marched towards the stairs and stopped when Michael walked in the front door without knocking.

"I hope it's okay." He glanced down at the

small bag in his hands. "I figured until she was well, I'd bunk here."

She smiled. "Perfect. It's okay, as long as you don't mind helping me move some furniture around."

He set his computer bag down at the base of the stairs and followed her up the stairs. She'd removed all the paintings that lined the stairs the second night she'd been there. They just creeped her out as did all the old-fashioned paintings her mother had hung around the house. Now the walls were completely bare, at least until she found several large pieces of bright art to hang on them.

"What do you need moved?" He followed her into her parents' room.

"Everything." She turned and smiled at him. "So, the question is, do you want to do it now, or later?"

He glanced around and sighed. "Well, I'm already dirty, so now is good."

"Perfect." She reached up on her toes and planted a big kiss on his lips.

Chapter Thirteen

Two hours later, she glanced around her new room and smiled. "Wow, what a difference." He took her shoulders in his hands and pulled her back into his chest.

"Now it's mine." She smiled. Her parents had had thick dark curtains on every window. Once they had removed all those, they swapped out her mattress with her parents and moved the bed into a corner. She found two nightstands and a dresser in her grandmother's room that went perfectly with the bed. The walls upstairs had only ever been painted white. Michael had run next door and brought over the rest of his paint. They had enough to paint one wall, which acted as an accent wall. One the paint dried, she hung a large mirror that she'd found in the attic over the dresser. It went perfectly with the darker wall.

She thought about going into town and looking for some local art to hang on the other walls.

She'd moved all of her things into the bigger bathroom and had tossed all of her parents' clothing into her grandmother's room so she could go through it later.

Her old room sat empty now and she thought briefly about turning it into an office or workout room at some later time.

"How about a long, hot shower," he whispered next to her ear. "After I check on the dog that is."

"Rose."

"Hmm?" He turned her around and wrapped his arms around her.

"It's her favorite smell. I think she'll like it." She smiled and wrapped her arms around his neck.

"Rose it is." He leaned down and kissed her. "I'll go check up on Rose, then we can shower and after…" His eyes moved to the fresh bed.

"Sounds good." She moaned with excitement.

When he disappeared down the hallway, she glanced around once more. She'd never really been allowed in her parents' room before. So mentally, she had no problem with taking it over as her own. Actually, she believed it would help her get over their loss. Not that she was doing much grieving, but she had thought about them frequently since arriving back home.

She still avoided going into town down the road they'd crashed on and had only traveled it once, the day she'd arrived home. She didn't like the energy or thoughts that had crossed her when she'd passed by the spot where they had died.

She didn't know what she would do if she happened to see them.

She felt a shiver run down her spine and purposely walked into the bathroom to turn on the hot water. Peeling off her clothes, she stepped into the spray and moaned with pleasure.

"Sounds like you're having fun without me," Michael observed from outside the glass doors.

"Why don't you come in here and see for yourself," she teased.

When the door opened, she smiled and then lost her breath at the sight of him, completely naked and hard. He was standing there on the shower mat, just staring at her. His eyes heated as they roamed slowly over every curve.

Her eyes did the same, taking in the muscles, the sexy trail of dark hair that traveled down the lower part of his belly button to his hardness, which jumped when her eyes landed on it.

"Beautiful," she whispered. "I didn't get to enjoy looking much last night," she said as he slowly moved into the shower. "Now I want…"

She stood back, making more room for him under the spray. "I want to enjoy you." She trailed a finger over his chest. She watched his eyes close when she flicked a finger over one of his nipples. Then her finger followed the trail of light hair down his chest, over the ripples of muscle, dipped in briefly to his bellybutton, then gripped him firmly with her hand.

His head rolled back under the spray as a low moan escaped his closed lips. She enjoyed exploring him slowly with her fingertips, feeling each muscle jump under her touch. He kept his head back and his eyes closed as she wrapped her fingers around him, then his brown eyes met hers.

"How much do you want me?" she asked. "Remember, I can't read you." A smile played on her lips.

"Too much." He groaned. "Too damn much." He took a step towards her until her back touched the cool tile wall of the shower. Then his hands started their own tour of her body. He reached up and poured some shampoo on his hands, lathered it up, then slowly moved his hands in circles as he touched every part of her.

"There's something about how I feel when I'm with you," he said as his hands continued their path. "Something that just clicks, like this is where I'm supposed to be." He leaned down and pushed his body against hers until she was the one moaning.

"Yes," she panted.

When her eyes met his, she knew the exact feeling he was talking about. It was like sparks of warmth radiated from him into her. Her heart felt like it was finally beating for the first time. Her nails dug softly into his skin.

"Michael." She waited until he looked into her eyes. "There's a storm that's been brewing in me for years, and now that you're here... I'm calm." She wrapped her arms around his shoulders and placed a soft kiss on his lips.

His fingers stilled on her as his mouth took over exploring her. "There's so much we can do together," he said against her skin. "I want to take my time and enjoy every minute." He rained kisses down to her shoulder. "Every glorious inch of this sexy body." His hands started moving again.

"You're torturing me," she burst out after a moment, causing a smirk to cross his face.

"And enjoying it."

Her eyes narrowed as her hands started moving over him again. "Two can play at this game." She watched his eyes heat as her fingers found him, harder than before.

"Now you're playing with fire," he warned.

"Good, I like it hot." She pushed gently until their positions were reversed and he was the one leaning against the wall. She plastered her body against his, used her mouth and hands until she felt his body shiver with want.

Just when she was on the verge of losing control, Michael pushed her away, turned her until her back was fitted against his body and in the next moment, plunged into her with so much force, she had to grip the tile wall to steady herself.

The sheer joy of having him fill her had her laughing and groaning at the same time.

"More?" he asked against her shoulder. "Tell me you want more." This time it came out as a growl.

"Yes," she begged. "More." She held on as her body arched, ached, and responded to his every move.

His mouth moved over her shoulder as his hands reached around and cupped her, causing her to build faster than before. She screamed his name as light exploded behind her closed eyes. Her entire body tensed with the power that shocked her, starting at her core and radiating throughout every ounce of her body.

When her mind finally settled, she realized that he was leaning heavily on her, his hands firmly stopping her from melting to the floor.

"Is that normal?" he grunted next to her skin.

"What? The earth-shattering sex?" she whispered, unable to control the shivers that still radiated through her.

She felt him chuckle against his skin. "That and I am pretty sure we just made the entire state light up." He gently moved her until she stood once more and he held her against his chest. "What do you say we move this party into that soft bed so we don't end up killing ourselves in here."

She mustered up enough strength to nod against his chest.

He pulled her from the warm shower, wrapped a large towel around her, and then spent a moment drying himself off. She leaned against the countertop and watched him in the simple task, feeling enamored at how beautiful he was, how lucky she was to have him here, in her place, wanting to be with her. Desiring her. Shattering her. She smiled slightly.

"What?" He'd been watching her and moved closer.

"I was just thinking how beautiful you are." She tucked the towel more tightly around her, then wrapped her arms around him once more.

"You do know how to make a guy blush." He hoisted her up and carried her into the bedroom, where he dropped her gently on the bed and crawled in next to her. "Sleep." She shut her eyes.

"I don't think I can. For some reason…" Her words dropped away when his hand covered her breast. Then his lips slowly moved over her shoulder. His hand moved slightly, massaging her shoulder, down her arm, over her ribs, then settled lightly on her stomach.

His lips soothed her, calmed her, until she felt her heart settle, her mind clear. Suddenly her mind was drifting as she listened to his slow breath next to her. His arms tightened around her as she settled deeper under the blankets, his warmth and comfort closing around her.

She slipped easily into dreams full of Michael's soft kisses and heated touch.

***

Mike woke when the cell phone he'd set on her nightstand chimed. Glancing over, he noticed they'd drifted off for almost a full hour. He'd set the alarm to wake them so they would have plenty of daylight to explore the silo.

He'd even brought several items they would need for the trip: more flashlights, some flares, a first aid kit, and other smaller items. His father had taught him and Ethan early in their childhood to be prepared. What his father had left out, the military and police force had filled in.

He shifted lightly, not wanting to wake Xtina up just yet. Instead, he pulled his cell phone out and did a few quick searches on missile silos in Georgia.

Apparently there were five documented sites, all built in the sixties. It even included longitude and latitude locations. Looking at maps, he found the one they had stumbled across and wondered how many others in town knew that it existed.

More important, why had his ghost—he glanced over at Xtina—his "not a ghost" wanted them to go down there.

He read up a little on what they might expect when they traversed down the ladder, but there were so many different options, and he didn't know if any of them applied to this silo.

He hadn't been looking too hard last night, but he was pretty sure there had been several tunnels leading away from the area in different directions.

Most of the plans he found online showed several bunker areas sprouting from the main silo, which should have had two large hydraulic doors covering it. How long those doors had been open, and how they had gotten opened in the first place, was a mystery to him.

One thing was clear—he wasn't the first one to go down there since the bunker had been abandoned. He'd seen graffiti all over the walls.

His phone buzzed again and he knew it was time to wake Xtina. Rolling over, his eyes moved over her face and he felt his heart skip. Her hair lay on the pillow in a messy array of curls. Her dark eyelashes lay on her flawless cheeks.

He twisted around until he laid next to her once more, his hands pulling her closer. She shifted in sleep, then slowly opened her eyes.

"Hey," she said quietly as a smile grew on her

lips.

"Hey, did you get enough sleep?" he asked, watching her green eyes focus on him.

She nodded, then yawned. "Yes." She stretched her arms over her head and then reached for the blankets, remembering that she'd fallen asleep naked. He tugged them farther down her body, causing her to squeal with laughter.

"Hey, I don't mess with you when you're…" Her words fell away as he quickly covered her with his equally naked body.

"You were saying?" he said between kisses.

"Mmm." She shook her head slowly as her arms wrapped around his waist.

He knew they were going to lose some daylight, but he figured it would be well worth it.

A little over a half an hour later, he was thankful he'd allowed them that extra time. His body felt relaxed and his mind was a little more in control. He could tell that Xtina felt the same as they got dressed in silence.

When they went downstairs, they were both shocked to see Rose standing by the back door, desperately wanting to go out.

"Do you think she'll be okay going out by herself?" he asked Xtina, who was already opening the door.

"She'll be fine. She already thinks of you as

hers." She smiled.

His eyebrows shot up. "Me?"

Xtina nodded. "Yeah, dogs own their humans, not the other way around. Remember, they're pack animals."

She reached for his jacket, the one she'd worn last night, from the hook by the back door. "She'll want some of the leftover turkey from the fridge." She glanced at him from over her shoulder.

"Does she also prefer me to feed her?" he asked as he walked over to the fridge and pulled out a Tupperware of what he assumed was turkey meat.

"No, she just likes having a man serve her." She laughed when she heard a soft whine from the other side of the door. "Back so soon?" she asked when Rose walked in like she owned the place. She went immediately over to Mike, who was already setting some of the container contents in the bowl they had fed her in last night.

Xtina walked over and took a larger bowl they had filled with water and refilled it for the dog.

They ate the rest of the turkey meat in sandwiches and each had a soda that Jessie had stocked in her fridge. When they were done, he turned to her.

"Ready?" He picked up the backpack full of the items he'd need from the counter.

She took a deep breath then slowly nodded. "Do you think we have everything we'll need?" She bit her bottom lip.

"I think so." He reached over and took her hand. "Hey, if you don't want…"

"No!" she jumped in a little too quickly. "I'll be fine." She pulled on the coat and walked to the door.

Chapter Fourteen

*T*hey made their way quickly to the spot. The trek was easier since they could see a path, and in less than half an hour, they stood at the large opening.

Now she was wondering how Rose had fallen down the hole in the first place.

"Does it look different today?" Michael asked. When she turned towards him, he had a frown on his face.

"Yeah, I was just thinking the same thing."

There were two very large, very heavy looking doors covering the silo area. One was cracked open slightly, but nothing like what she remembered from last night.

"Maybe she had something to do with it being open," she suggested.

"Either way, we're going to have to pry it open a little more." He removed his backpack and set it down on the ground.

"What about…" She looked around. "Do you think there's another way in?"

He thought about it. "Most of the silos I researched had a separate entrance for the bunker." He glanced around. "We're looking for a small building." He glanced around. "It would be on this land, not the farm." He nodded towards the Miller's place.

"Okay, so we split up and look." She looked back down at the hole.

"Agreed." He took up his bag again and nodded. "I'll head this way." He nodded towards the woods. "You take that way." He nodded in the opposite direction.

She took off in her direction. The property was bigger than she'd expected. She'd assumed that the building would be fairly close to the silo, but in the end, it was almost a full mile away. She called out to Michael, who immediately responded, as if he'd followed her.

"I ran into a fence and figured it would be in this direction since there was no other place to go my way," he explained.

The small building was made completely of

cement cinder blocks. The door, a thick metal one with a huge lock, that had been jimmied opened, what appeared to be years ago.

"So, this is how they got in," he murmured.

"Who?" She turned to him, her head tilted slightly.

He shrugged. "Well, I assume the kids that spray-painted their names at the bottom of the silo." He took out his flashlight and handed her one. "Ready?"

She nodded, then followed him through the doorway. The dark swallowed them whole.

"I can't believe how dark it is down here," she said after they had traversed down three different sets of metal staircases.

She was a little breathless by the time they reached the bottom.

"No natural light. They had to keep things sealed off." He glanced over at her and shined the flashlight at his face. "Just in case they dropped the bombs…" he said in a spooky voice as he wiggled his eyebrows.

"You're such a dork." She laughed at him.

He was right, the walls were covered in old spray paint.

"When was the last time you think someone was down here?" she asked.

"I'm guessing 1992." He pointed to the wall.

212

"It's the latest date I've seen." He shined his light on the walls and she realized he was right. There were dates ranging from the mid-seventies all the way to the early nineties. Had her parents ever snuck in here themselves? She shook the thought from her mind.

Her eyes scanned the colorful language covering the walls. Her parents, much like most people who grew up in Hidden Creek, had been raised very religious. No way they would have been involved with something like this.

They reached the base of the staircase and glanced around. Two long tunnels split off in opposite directions. One had a bright red metal door at the end, a shiny silver lock on the handle. The other tunnel went farther than both of their flashlights could see.

She felt a shiver race through her. "You feel that?" he almost whispered it.

"Yeah." Her eyes zeroed in on the shorter hallway. "I..." She felt her stomach roll.

She moved slowly to the opening of the circular hallway. Instantly, a flood of blinding flashes temporarily blinded her. Falling to her knees, she felt an onslaught of emotions hit her, causing her to hunch over and lose the contents of her stomach.

She felt Michael holding her, rubbing her back and pulling her long ponytail aside.

"Mike," she cried out as another wave of lights

blinded her. This time, she knew she was in trouble, since her eyes had been closed tight. "I…"

She felt herself being picked up and quickly carried up the stairs they had just climbed. The pain in her head lessened the higher they went.

"There's something there," she said when he reached the top and set her back down in the soft grass. She lay down, her eyes closed to the brightness of the sunlight.

The warmth of its rays felt so wonderful, she imagined spending an hour there, just getting warm again.

"Something as in…" His voice was close to her and she could hear him trying to get his breath back under control after racing up three flights of stairs, carrying her.

She shook her head, not wanting to open her eyes again yet. "Something I've never experienced before." She felt a shiver race through her.

"Will you be okay?"

"Yes," she said hesitantly, opening her eyes. "You don't plan on…" She stopped when he turned back towards the door.

"I left my pack down there." He turned to her again and she could see the worry in his eyes. "I don't want to leave you, but I would like a chance to do a little exploring."

She sat up, tucking her knees to her chest. "I'll be fine." She pulled out a bottle of water from her own pack and drank until she felt a little steadier. "Go." She closed her eyes. "See what you can." She reached out and took his hand before he could move away. "Be careful. There's something down there."

"Alive?" His eyes moved to the door again.

"No...yes." She shook her head. "I don't know. Something else."

"Right." He nodded, then leaned down and placed a kiss on the top of her head. "Be right back."

She watched him disappear and then leaned back down on the ground. She stared at the clouds going by as she counted the seconds he was gone and tried to separate all the images she'd seen.

***

Mike stopped and picked up his pack, then stood at the mouth of the hallway for almost an entire minute before he took his next step.

Nothing. Not even a shiver up his spine. He took another, then another until he was at the end of the very long hallway. It too split off into two different directions. He decided to take the shorter route first, which led into a smaller room with six bunk beds and a small desk area, probably used to house the employees. He turned around and went down the longer hallway.

Once again, it split off and he found himself in a large room that appeared to be a common room

215

with a small kitchen area off to one side. Most of the furniture had been removed, except for an old sofa and desk.

As with the rest of the place, the walls were covered in spray paint. The smell of the place was almost overpowering. Dust, animal feces, dirt, and rust.

Still, nothing out of the ordinary. He moved back to the main hallway and met two large metal doors with the year 1993 and several initials painted on them.

As with the rest of the rooms, he pulled out his phone and snapped a few pictures. He pushed the door open slightly, and the smell and sound of dripping water hit him.

The room opened to a large, three- story area. Yellow metal scaffolding hung all over the place. Here, there was no paint. He snapped a few pictures, then walked closer to the edge and glanced over. The area easily went down three more stories. At the bottom, the entire floor was covered in dark water. He saw a set of circular stairs in the corner and snapped some more pictures before heading down them.

The next floor had what he assumed were old computer racks. They were massive empty metal shells. The ceiling and walls were covered in cables. It must have been some sort of command center. After taking a few more pictures, he headed down one more level.

When his feet hit water, he stopped. There should be five more steps. Which meant he was going to get wetter than he'd first thought. Setting his bag down on a dry stair, he removed his jacket and set it on top of the bag. Then he stepped into the cold water and shivered.

This floor was shaped as the floor above. He walked a few yards down the hallway until it opened up into the silo area. He could see the sunlight coming through the slight slit in the metal doors.

He thought about calling out to Xtina, then remembered she was probably still back at the other entrance. He looked around for a switch or a way to open the hydraulic doors, but didn't see anything. It was probably better to keep them shut, anyway. He didn't want any other animals to fall in like Rose had.

He stopped at the railing and glanced up. He was standing on the floor of the silo now, where he had found Rose. It was currently covered in water, probably from the rain he'd heard as they had slept.

Taking his phone out, he snapped a few pictures, then tucked it back into his pocket.

He looked up again and frowned. The metal ladder he'd used last night was still there. Everything else was the same, except the water.

Since he couldn't go any further, he returned to

the stairs and found his way back up to the exit. When he opened the door, Xtina rushed over to him and wrapped her arms around him.

"I was so worried about you," she said into his chest.

"It's okay." He chuckled. "Nothing weird happened."

She nodded. "Okay, good." She glanced at her watch. "It's going to be dark soon. And Jess is supposed to come by." She hugged him again. "You can fill us both in then."

He nodded. "I'd like a shower beforehand." He nodded down to his wet feet.

She took his hand. "Was it spooky?" He felt a shiver run through her.

"No, the only spooky part was when you had your…"

"Fit?" she supplied, causing him to worry even more.

"Whatever you want to call it." He took her hand up to his lips. "You okay?"

She nodded as they made their way back across the field. They walked in silence until they reached her yard and both noticed the car in the driveway.

"Who do you suppose that is?" Michael asked.

She turned to him and sighed. "I would think that it's your brother."

He felt his stomach roll and his hand tightened on Xtina's.

"I had hoped not to have to deal with this so soon. I haven't even talked to my folks yet."

"Easy. I'm sure he has as many questions and hurt feelings about all this as you do." She pushed closer and kissed him. "Try to think of this from his point of view. You've done some research, so maybe he's done his own and you two can compare notes." She stepped back and took his hand, then started pulling him towards the house.

He felt conflicted, but knew she was probably right. After all, how long could he avoid the man? They lived in the same small town. Hell, the guy was probably going to be chief of police soon.

When they reached the front of her house, Jacob got out of the car and started walking towards them.

"Hey." His eyes focused on Xtina's instead of Mike's.

"Hi." She smiled at him, causing a split second of jealousy to surface, but Mike quickly squashed it.

"I hope it's okay that I stopped by." His eyes moved over to Mike's, then back towards Xtina's.

"Sure," she started to say. Mike watched her rub the side of her head as he felt his stomach growl.

"Why don't we head inside. I'm starved," he

interrupted. He took her hand and started walking towards the door.

"Don't you lock your house?" Jacob said when they pushed the door open. They were met with barks and the sound of dog paws rushing towards them.

"Rose, it's just us," Xtina called out, then smiled when the dog came rushing around the corner and happily greeted them. Xtina turned to Jacob. "I had a new security system installed yesterday." She winked as she bent down to pat the dog, then laughed when Rose licked her face.

"Yes, still..." Jacob glanced around quickly. "I'm sorry about your folks."

"Thank you." She stood up and wrapped her arms around herself.

"I'll get a fire going." Mike set his pack down and moved over to start building the fire.

"Would you like something to drink?" Xtina asked Jacob.

"No, I'm fine." Mike noticed that Jacob continued to walk around the room, like he was taking stock of it, much as he had done that first night.

"Well, I'm going to go grab some water." Her eyes met Mike's and he knew that she was leaving the pair alone so they could talk.

"Actually," Jacob broke in, "I was hoping to talk to you."

"You will." Her smile didn't show behind her eyes. "First, I'd like some aspirin. I've been fighting a headache." She turned and quickly left the room. Rose trailed behind her.

"So, you and her..." Jacob broke in after Mike had the fire going.

He didn't respond, just continued to look at... his brother. He shook that thought off. It was too early to jump to conclusions. Even though he trusted what Xtina said... he was a facts kind of man.

"Listen." Jacob finally sat down across from him, his elbows propped up on his knees, much like Mike was doing. "I know this is weird, and to be honest, I'm not sure I believe what she says either." He nodded towards the kitchen door. "But, you have to admit, there's a slight possibility that you and I are brothers."

Mike sighed and rested back in the chair. "Yeah." He thought about all the research he'd done, and all the research he still wanted to do. "She hasn't been wrong once. Not since I've met her."

"You moved into town almost a year ago, right?" Jacob asked.

"Yeah."

"If it's okay, I'd like to ask you a few other questions." He pulled out a small notepad from his back jean pocket.

This time it was his turn to rub at his temple and he desperately wished for a beer. Looking across the room, he noticed the same determined look on Jacob's face that he saw when he looked in his own mirror every day.

"Shoot," he said after a moment.

Chapter Fifteen

Xtina wasted as much time in the kitchen as she could. She put together a pot of spaghetti and made a shopping list. She even spent some time looking in the laundry room for old socks she could tie up as toys for Rose and played fetch with her in the back yard until dinner was ready.

When she finally walked into the living room to let the two men know it was time to eat, they were both laughing and looked a lot more relaxed around one another. Earlier, they had looked like two roosters stuck in the same hen house.

"Dinner's ready," she said, handing Michael a cold beer. She took a sip from the one she'd been nursing for a while.

"Thanks," he said as Jacob stood up. His eyes

moved over the two of them as she sat on the edge of the chair's armrest.

"Why don't you stay?" she suggested out of the blue. "I've made enough food."

"No. I should—" He started to say.

"Stay," Mike broke in. "Unless you have somewhere else to be?"

She watched his eyes and knew the second he made up his mind to stay.

"Good, how about a beer and some spaghetti?" she asked, jumping up from her spot next to Mike.

They moved into the kitchen. She'd set the table and the warmth from the old stove had made the room cozy. It smelled of warm bread and Italian spices.

She set the pan of spaghetti on the table and placed the French bread she'd warmed in the oven in the middle.

"Do you want to tell me about what you found at the silo?" she finally asked after everyone's plates were full of food.

Mike's eyes moved over to hers and she could see the warning behind them.

"Silo?" Jacob asked.

"I had hoped to keep our little adventure of breaking and entering on government property off the table while there was law enforcement sitting at it," Mike said, taking another sip of his beer.

"The one on the property next to the Miller place?" Jacob asked.

Xtina chuckled. "Does everyone in town know about the place other than us?"

"How is it that you were raised here and didn't know about it? I mean, it's what… two miles from your house?"

Mike shifted when she nudged him under the table.

"I wasn't allowed out much." Her eyes moved to her plate and she felt Mike's hand wrap around hers.

"Her parents were… very protective," Mike supplied. Xtina tried to hold in a snort.

"Kids have been sneaking into that place since the seventies," Jacob said as he finished his plate of food. "My dad had to install new locks back in the day after all the trouble."

"Trouble?" she asked.

Jacob didn't have a chance to answer because Rose jumped up and started barking happily as she ran circles around the kitchen table.

"Hello?" Jessie called out as she opened the front door.

"Back here," Xtina replied.

Rose rushed towards the door to greet Jessie,

who stooped down and gave the dog a treat from the box of treats she held in her hands.

A wave of power hit Xtina and suddenly so many things were clear.

"I brought you a few other things for her." Jessie stood, smiling. The smile fell away when she noticed Jacob sitting at the table. He was leaning back in the chair and taking a swallow of his beer.

"What is he doing here?" Jessie frowned.

"He's having dinner." Xtina stood, then took the box of treats from her friend, along with a small box of dog toys. She whispered, "Be nice."

"Actually, I was just…" Jacob started to say, but then Xtina turned to him and glared until he sat back down without another word.

The room was silent as she cleared the food and empty plates away. Then she turned to Jessie. "Sit. We need to talk."

She looked around the room. She couldn't explain it, but suddenly, there was more energy in the room than she'd ever felt in her entire life.

When she sat down at the table, she took Mike's hand in her own and reached for Jessie's. To her friend's credit, she didn't hesitate and took her hand in her own.

She nodded towards the empty hands until everyone completed the circle. When the last hands were connected, a jolt rushed through her entire system and she felt a bolt of lightning spread behind her eyes. She must have cried out in pain, because suddenly Mike was there, holding her. "NO!" she cried out. "Don't break the circle."

"What the hell?" she heard from Jacob.

She'd been flooded with so many images she had to find out more. "Please." She kept her eyes closed as she held out her hand once more.

The room was silent as Mike sat down again and took her hand. She felt his hesitation, but then his fingers wrapped around hers.

This time she braced for it. Her eyes opened upon the connection and before them stood the woman, floating softly above her kitchen table. In broad daylight.

***

Mike watched in horror as all the color drained from Xtina's face. Her eyes grew bigger, greener, and became unfocused.

He was pretty sure they were the only ones seeing the figure until his eyes moved around to Jacob's and Jessie's faces. They too were pale faced and wide-eyed.

"You can see her?" he asked softly.

Both of them nodded in unison.

"The time is near," Xtina said. Everyone's eyes moved to her. "Time to make things right. Time for the payment you promised."

"What payment?" he asked after a moment of silence as the air around them crackled.

But Xtina was not responding. Her eyes focused on the image before them. Suddenly, the figure pulsed and blinked until it was gone.

"Two more are needed," she whispered. He watched in horror as she slumped over.

He caught her before she hit her head. "Take her upstairs," Jessie said, rushing to her side. "She'll need water." She moved over to the sink and followed him upstairs.

When he set her gently on her bed, Jessie set the items down on the nightstand.

"Wow, I like what you've done up here." She glanced around.

"Is she going to be okay?" Jacob asked from the doorway.

"She'll be fine." Jess turned towards him, her eyes narrowing slightly. "You can wait downstairs."

Mike turned to her. "We should all let her rest." He felt her steady heartbeat under his fingers as he ran his hand gently over her wrist.

"She'll sleep for a while." Jess rested a hand on his shoulder.

They left the room, and Mike shut the door

behind them quietly.

"She'll be okay." Jess touched his arm again. He watched Jacob's eyebrows shoot up at the tenderness Jess showed him.

Without saying a word, he moved back down the stairs.

"Now, will someone please tell me what the hell just happened?" Jacob said at the base of the stairs.

For the next half hour, he explained what had taken place since he'd moved here. He filled them both in on what he'd found in the silo, then Jess pulled out the yearbook and showed him the photo of her parents and Xtina's. He was shocked to see his own parents in the mix a few pages later.

"They must have all been friends," Jessie said, smiling. "I guess that explains a lot."

"Yeah? Like why we all just saw a ghost floating in the kitchen?" Jacob broke in, taking another sip of his new beer.

"It's not a ghost." He chuckled when he said it, then walked to the fridge and got himself another beer. The cold liquid hit his dry throat.

"Then what the hell do you call that?" Jacob motioned to the table.

"I think Xtina called it an entity," Jess stated.

"Same thing." Jacob glared at her.

Just what was between the pair was beyond him, but he was starting to get a headache and wanted to go upstairs and check on Xtina.

"Look!" Jessie shouted, causing him to jump. Her eyes moved up to his. "Byron."

"Byron?" he asked, then remembered the name she'd changed the night of Xtina's parents' funeral. "Byron?" He pulled the yearbook out of Jessie's hand and looked down at the image of his parents, Xtina's parents, and another couple, a blonde woman with silver blue eyes and a young man, a lot taller than his own father.

Underneath the photo it said *Byron Garrett*.

"Who is Byron Garrett?"

"I don't know." Jessie frowned over his shoulder.

"Who the hell cares," Jacob added, causing Jessie to frown at him.

"Listen, I'm kind of beat." His eyes moved to the ceiling where he could hear the shower running upstairs. "I'd like to go check on Xtina."

Jacob nodded. "How about we meet later this week?" he asked Mike.

"I'll come into the station." There were a few other things he wanted to talk to Jacob about and he figured he'd make it professional instead of personal.

Jacob nodded, then glanced over at Jessie. "Night."

Jessie waited a few minutes. "I'll leave this here." She set the yearbook down on the table and then glanced over at the door.

"I'm sure he's gone by now," Mike supplied.

Jessie rolled her eyes. "The man is arrogant." Mike's eyebrows rose. "Long story. Night. Tell Xtina I'll call her tomorrow."

He nodded, then watched her leave. He looked down at Rose, who had been sitting by his side for a while. "I suppose you want out." He glanced at her empty food and water bowl. The dog had quickly wolfed down a large bowl of food as they had talked. Walking over, he opened the back door, then refilled her water bowl. When he heard a small scratching noise from the back door, he opened it and Rose walked in. She took a few laps of water, then made her way towards the stairs.

He locked the doors, then climbed up the stairs to join Xtina.

When he walked in the bedroom, she was just coming out of the shower.

"Did everyone leave?" she asked. Her coloring was back. She had a soft white robe wrapped around her as she used a towel to dry her hair.

"Yes." He walked over and wrapped his arms around her. "You okay?"

She nodded into his shoulder. "Much better." He felt her shiver just before her arms wrapped around her. "She's angry. She's never been angry

232

before."

"At us?" he asked, moving her back a step so he could see her eyes.

"No." She slowly shook her head. "I don't think so. It was more at... the circumstance." She sighed. "How about some ice cream?" she asked out of the blue.

"Maybe later. I'm going to head in and shower." He felt the layer of dirt and grime from climbing inside the silo suddenly. Not to mention the sore muscles from all the tension of the day.

"Shower." She smiled. "Then we can enjoy some dessert." She leaned up and kissed him quickly, then escaped his arms and disappeared out the door.

He peeled off his clothes, tossed them in the hamper, and climbed into the hot shower. When he stuck his head under the water, images of today passed through his mind.

What did the silo have to do with the woman? What debt needed to be paid? Was it something to do with their parents?

There was no doubt in his mind that the three couples had known one another. After all, they were all in the same high school together.

He groaned when he realized it was time he called his parents. He groaned even louder when he realized that if he mentioned Jacob, they would probably move their visit up.

When he climbed out of the shower, he could hear Xtina and Rose downstairs and picked up his cell phone to make one of the most awkward phone calls of his life.

His father answered on the third ring.

"Hey, son, we were just talking about our trip out there." His father sounded excited. "We haven't been back since our twentieth reunion a few years ago."

"Dad, can you put Mom on too?" he asked. His father's voice was now tinged with worry.

"Sure, is something wrong?"

"Just put me on speaker." He held his breath as he heard his father moving the phone around.

"I'm here, Michael." His mother's voice sounded close. "What's going on? You haven't heard from Ethan, have you?"

"No. But I have to ask you…" He took a deep breath. "Did you guys have a baby boy before us?"

The line was silent.

"Mom? Dad?" He checked his phone to make sure the connection was still good.

"What's this all about?" It was his father who asked.

"Just answer, yes or no."

"Michael." He could tell his mother was crying and knew then that it was true.

234

"Why?" he asked, his heart breaking slightly.

"We…" his mother started, but then his father broke in.

"We were young." He took the phone off speaker and he could hear his father comforting his mother. "We were too young. Back then… our parents thought it was best if we gave the baby up for adoption."

"Did you know he was raised in Hidden Creek?"

"No." His father's voice sounded sad. "We didn't know anything about the adoption family. Our parents took care of everything." He sighed, then spoke to his mother. "Why are you bringing this up now?"

"Because I've met him." He wondered if he should tell his parents everything. "I live in the same town." He hadn't realized that his voice had risen, until Xtina's hand rested on his shoulder softly.

Closing his eyes, he took a few breaths. "Jacob is on the police force here." He turned slightly as Xtina sat next to him on the bed.

"Jacob?" He heard his mother repeat the name. "How…" Suddenly the phone was put back on speaker. "How do you know it's him?"

"Because…" He looked over at Xtina and thought for a brief moment of explaining everything to them, but then shook his head.

"Because we look alike," he lied slightly. Only slightly, since it was sort of true, most of it. The fact that Jacob was almost a spitting image of his father, he kept to himself.

The line was silent for a while.

"We're heading down there first thing in the morning," his father said.

"Fine." He reached for Xtina's hand and felt her tense at his touch, so he dropped her hand and looked over at her. Her face had gone pale again. "Dad, I have to go."

"We'll see you around noon," he answered, then broke the connection.

"What?" he asked, turning to her after he tossed his phone down.

"They had no choice." He watched a tear slide down her face. "Their parents..." She shook her head. "I didn't see it before." She wrapped her arms around him. "They were forced to give him up." More tears slid down her face. "They wanted him as much as they wanted you." Her eyes moved to him. "Don't hate them. They're suffering as much as you are."

He held her close as he took it all in. He had a brother. Another one. A big brother. He'd been the oldest sibling for as long as he could remember. Even though Ethan and he were twins, he'd always thought of himself as the big brother.

But now, everything had changed. It didn't

matter that he hadn't been raised side by side with the man, he was family. Period.

He glanced towards the phone and thought about texting Ethan, but he knew that his brother was too deep in his mission to have a phone on him. Besides, he didn't know when he'd see him or hear from him again and he didn't want that to be the first news to reach him after spending weeks out of touch.

He fell backwards, taking Xtina with him until she settled on his chest.

"How about that ice cream?" she asked, nodding towards the tray of dessert on the nightstand.

"Yeah." He brushed his hands through her hair. "I suppose I could go for something sweet." He leaned down and placed his lips over hers softly. "After." He trailed his mouth over her face, kissing her eyes closed.

He needed the slowness, the softness of her to heal all the hurt that had built up inside him. Remembering seeing her pale, shaking with fear, made him go slower, made his hands and fingers gentler as he moved over her pale skin.

Looking into those sea green eyes of hers, knowing that they saw more than he could ever imagine, made him take his time pleasing her. He wanted to show her how he felt, since he knew she couldn't sense it from him.

So many emotions had swelled up inside him that when they lay naked and intertwined, he allowed the words to slip from his lips as he entered her slowly.

Chapter Sixteen

They needed to talk about so much. She rolled over, feeling her entire body still vibrating from everything Mike had just done to her.

"I think the ice cream melted."

"It's probably a puddle after all the heat we just generated," he joked back and she was glad he'd chosen to play it easy.

His hand settled on her bare back and she closed her eyes, wanting to hold on to that moment forever.

"Mike." She turned, looking down at him. His dark lashes were resting on his cheeks. When his eyes slid open, she knew they would have to talk about what he'd said.

"I…" She shook her head. "I can't allow myself to love." She felt the stab in her heart. "It's not in my cards." She stood up and watched his hand drop away from her.

"What do you mean?" His face went blank as he sat up slightly, resting back against the headboard.

"Love isn't for people like me." She reached down and picked up the robe he'd tossed onto the ground after he'd slowly peeled it from her earlier. She wrapped the softness around her, then hugged herself to try and get warm. Glancing over, she noticed that the apple pie and ice cream still looked good enough to eat. "Here." She handed him a bowl. "Let's enjoy this before it melts." She took her own bowl and sat next to him.

"You can't avoid this forever," he said after shoveling a bite of pie into his mouth.

"I know." She kept her eyes glued to the bowl of dessert. "Just not tonight." She felt her energy levels fade further.

His hand reached out for hers. "I'll give you tonight." He took her hand up to his mouth and placed a soft kiss on her knuckles, sending warmth and pain throughout her entire body.

That night, her dreams were full of images of pain, sorrow, loneliness, and love. She knew in her heart that none of it was her own, but images left over from her experience from the previous day.

241

When she woke, the bed was empty and the sheets were cold. When she looked around, she saw the note on her nightstand.

I have some work to do on my house before my folks come today. Can you come over for dinner? I'd like you to meet them. See you around six... I know you don't want to hear it, but I love you. M

She tucked the note close to her heart as she sat down on the bed and tears rolled down her cheeks.

Love. She'd never believed she'd be allowed to have it. To feel it. To enjoy it. All her life she'd hidden from it. No, it had hidden from her. There had been a few times she'd believed she'd fallen in love. Joe. Billy. She sighed at all the disappointments she'd experienced over the years. How she'd tried to give them everything she had, only to come up short.

Was Mike different? Could she trust her own heart this time? He was different in many ways. For one, he was the only person she couldn't read. When she looked into his eyes, she could only see what he was thinking through her own eyes.

She likened the feeling to being blind, only seeing the world through sounds and feeling around in the dark. She wasn't used to it. But, she realized, it didn't scare her so much with Mike.

Maybe she trusted him more than she'd trusted Joe and Billy. She didn't think there was any way that Mike would end up being like either of those two. Especially Billy. She felt a shiver run up her back.

She blocked thoughts of her past from her mind as she went about her business. She had a long list of things she needed to get in town and decided to make the run first thing, since she was low on coffee and Rose was begging her for some more of the treats Jessie had brought last night. She knew it probably wasn't good for the dog to have so many, but she figured a woman could afford to indulge when she was expecting.

Her first stop, after grabbing a cup of coffee and a cinnamon roll, was the vet. Rose was a little jittery walking in, but hearing Xtina's voice seemed to soothe her down. Then she met the vet and relaxed completely. She could tell that Rose liked the woman immediately.

"I'll give her a full checkup," the vet, Reba, said. "If you have some other errands to run, it should take about an hour." She ran a hand over Rose's belly. "We'll give her an ultrasound to make sure everything's all good."

"Thank you, I've got some grocery shopping to do. I'll be back after." She glanced down at her watch and marked the time and then ran a hand over Rose. "I'll be back."

She smiled when Rose lapped at her in acceptance.

She walked the block to the grocery store, grabbed a cart, and pulled her list from her purse.

243

The last time she'd been in the store, she'd passed out. She still couldn't figure out why, other than fatigue.

Now, she was careful to keep a few feet away from others as she piled items into her cart. She picked out two dog beds, one for upstairs, the other for the kitchen area. Then came the dog food and more treats and toys. She spent more time on the pet aisle than shopping for herself.

By the time she was in line at the checkout, she was sure she was spending way too much money on the dog, but Rose was worth it.

"You're that girl," someone said from behind her. "Aren't you?"

She turned and saw several women around her age looking at her. They were standing at the checkout, but didn't have carts or baskets. Instead, they each had a magazine in their hands, like they had just grabbed it so they could talk to her.

One was a tall blonde woman who had a purse thrown over her shoulder that had probably cost as much as the taxes on her car had. The other, a smaller dark-haired woman, was wearing very impressive designer clothing and some of the tallest heels Xtina had ever seen.

"I'm sorry?" she asked, not sure what they were asking.

"The one that's working with the police on Laura's case," the dark-haired woman said.

She felt her entire body stiffen and she thought for a moment about leaving all her items in the cart and just leaving.

"I've been advised not to speak about—" she started. It was the truth. Jacob had asked her not to talk about the case to anyone.

"Christina, correct?" the blonde said, her eyes going to the other woman's. "That's her. I remember she was in my biology class."

Xtina remembered the pair now. Robin and Carly. The dynamic duo, as Xtina and Jessie used to call them. Wherever they were, trouble was bound to follow.

Instead of answering, Xtina turned around and focused on emptying her cart onto the conveyor belt.

"I heard that you accused Laura of killing her husband," one of them said behind her. "Even after she'd been attacked herself."

Xtina took a couple deep breaths to steady herself. She'd learned that the best way to handle people like them was to ignore them.

"You have some nerve accusing someone when you have no idea what you're talking about."

Xtina sped up unloading her items and tucked her purse tighter under her arm.

"We're talking to you," one of them said, then reached out and took Xtina by the shoulder. She

245

hadn't been prepared for the contact and when images flooded her mind, she felt her knees weaken and felt the sting of the floor as she fell forward.

Damn, she thought as she hit the ground. Not again.

She heard laughter, which shook her from the haze. Her hands and knees were burning as she looked up through her hair.

Both women stood over her, laughing down at her.

"I told you she was a freak," Robin said, her arms crossed over her chest as Carly looked on. Both women had smiles on their faces as Xtina stood up slowly.

"Still, it's better than what the two of you have going on." Xtina straightened up, her shoulders going back as she felt strength building inside her.

They chuckled. "And what would that be?" Carly asked.

"Oh, I think it would be obvious." Her eyes moved to the expensive purses and clothing. "You do know that internet fraud is a crime." She motioned to the expensive bags that had been bought online using fake information.

"It's still theft." She leaned closer. "Even if you have gotten away with it for years."

She turned and ignored the sounds of them gasping and groaning behind her.

"She can't know about that," she heard Carly tell Robin as they rushed out of the store.

"Are you okay, miss?" the clerk said. He was a younger man who appeared to be in high school.

"Yes, I'm fine." She smiled and dusted her hands, only then realizing that they were slightly bleeding. "If you can, will you wait until I grab a box of bandages?"

He nodded and she rushed back down the aisles until she had a box of bandages.

"Thanks," she said, setting the box down.

"If you want, I'll tell the police what happened."

She shook her head. "No need. Those two have been a pain to me since they were born." She smiled and waved her hand. "Besides, I think they'll be leaving me alone from here on out."

With her knees and hands hurting, she pushed the full cart towards her car and knew she'd just taken the first steps to securing her future in Hidden Creek. No longer was she going to be afraid of the people in it. No longer was she going to hide her true self from anyone.

She felt more powerful than she had in her entire life. Stronger. More sure, and most important, free. Free to finally be herself.

***

Mike finished setting up his guest room by

247

moving the furniture from the garage into the room and making the bed with the new sheets he'd bought a few weeks back. Then he moved into the kitchen. He'd hardly gotten anything done in the room in the past few days other than the flooring.

His cupboards had been delivered a few weeks back and sat in the garage, so he spent the next few hours carrying them in and installing them. The process was slow and he sure could have used a second pair of hands.

When there was a knock at his door, he called out for them to enter, just as he slammed his thumb with a hammer.

"Son of a…." he exclaimed.

"I wouldn't finish that if I were you. Not with the woman you're speaking of standing in the same room," his father said, smiling slightly.

"Hey." He set the hammer down and walked over to shake his dad's hand and receive a hug from his mother. He held on to her while she burst into tears. His eyes met his dad's over her head and he knew he'd better hold on to her, that she needed it.

"I'm sorry," she kept saying over and over. "I should have…" She cried into his shoulder as she continued to mumble into his chest.

"Mom." He held her. "It's okay. I think I understand." He hadn't realized that he was crying until his father handed him a napkin.

"Well, if you two are done sniffling about it," his father said, using a napkin himself, "can we sit down and have that talk?"

Two hours later, after a long talk over cold sandwiches, his father changed into some work clothes and helped him finish installing the cupboards.

"The countertops are being installed next week, so we'll have to deal with the boards." He nodded towards the plywood they had set atop the cupboards.

"It'll do," his mother said when she came back from the local store with a car full of groceries. "Now, you two go clean up while I get to work." She rolled up her sleeves and pushed them out of the room. "You stink." She smiled and then reached up and kissed them both on the cheek.

He'd always loved how well his family could bounce back from things. He'd never had to question if he was loved. All he had to do was look into his parents' faces.

He knew, after what Xtina had said, that they had been young and trusting. Too naive to really understand what they were doing, giving up a child at the tender age of sixteen or seventeen.

He took a deep breath. He'd never been in the position himself, but if he had… He thought about it as he showered. Would he have done the same?

He'd like to think no. But… children change

things. Sure, he'd always thought that someday he would have a family. But after the military and the police force, he'd put all that aside. Especially when he'd thought he was going crazy.

Now... his mind conjured up an image of children with sea green eyes and blonde curls running around. He hadn't realized he was smiling until he cut himself shaving and cursed under his breath.

Refocusing on the simple task, he finished his shower and put the thought of enjoying Xtina and his kids off to the future.

When he walked out, his house smelled better than it ever had. "My god!" he exclaimed as he walked into the room. His father was already sitting at the bar area, his elbows propped up on the plywood as he watched his wife cook. "I'd forgotten how wonderful your cooking smells."

His mother turned and smiled at him. "Good, now go and get the rest of the groceries from the back of my car." She winked at him. "I'm almost done here."

He groaned as he walked out. When he pulled the two paper bags from his parents' trunk, he noticed the white bouquet of flowers and smiled.

His mother thought of everything. He heard the barking first, then turned to see Xtina walk across the yard towards him. Rose made it to him first, so he bent down and spent a moment enjoying the dog kisses.

250

"She missed you," Xtina said, walking directly into his arms. She smiled as she kissed him slowly. He easily lost himself in her soft lips and buried his fingers into her softer hips.

"There, that will answer some questions they have." She nodded towards the house. He glanced over just in time to see both of his parents rush away from the window.

He laughed. "Here." He bent down and pulled out the flowers. "My mother." He nodded towards the house. "Not that I wouldn't have gotten you flowers on my own, but I've been busy today."

"Thank you." She buried her face in the flowers and when she leaned back, he swore to himself that he would buy her flowers every day if she would continue to smile like that.

"You look beautiful." He stepped back and took her hand. She was wearing a soft gray and coral sweater dress that reached to just above her knees.

She looked damn yummy. "Shall we go in?" he said after a moment.

She nodded, and he almost forgot the bags in the back of his parents' car.

"I hope it's okay that I brought Rose," she said. He'd forgotten about the dog, who sat on his front porch like she belonged there.

"Sure, my folks have two shih tzus. Ricky and Lucy."

Xtina smiled. She stopped outside the door and took a deep breath. "Okay, here we go."

He took her hand and raised it to his lips. "They are going to love you." He kissed her skin and felt her shiver. "Really."

She nodded, then he opened the door.

Chapter Seventeen

An hour later, it was clear his parents *did* like her. She had yet to touch them, other than a brief handshake, during which she'd done everything in her power to block any visions.

She'd been impressed with how much work Mike and his father had gotten done in the kitchen. Even with plywood for countertops, the place was looking pretty amazing.

His mother had made some of the best chicken she'd had in years. There was a light crust of oats and each breast lay in a bed of potatoes, veggies, and herbs. She could have eaten the entire platter.

They sat around the living room talking about Mike and Ethan's childhood and how the two of them got into as much trouble as they could.

It was nice listening to how normal his life had been and she tried not to continually compare it with her own screwed-up childhood. But as the evening went on, she was even more sure that she wasn't cut out to have any sort of "normal" anything. Her parents had seen to that.

Mike reached over and took her hand. He must have sensed her sadness, so she shifted her thoughts quickly.

"Michael tells me you two grew up around here?"

"Yes." They both glanced at one another. "Rusty and I met in high school here. My parents moved here when I was fifteen. Rusty lived here his entire life." She reached over and took her husband's hand.

"I don't know if Michael told you…"

"Dad," Mike broke in. "Xtina is the one that told me about Jacob."

Both of their eyes moved to hers.

And here it goes, she thought. All the normalcy in the evening would be gone. So much for ending the evening peacefully and happily.

She braced and Mike glanced over at her, feeling the tension in their joined hands.

"It's not my story to tell," he whispered. "It's up to you."

She slowly dropped his hand and leaned

255

forward.

"Susan?" She held out her hand waiting. "If you'd be willing…"

Mike's mother's eyes moved to her hands, then back up towards Mike.

"Go ahead, Mom. I think you'll enjoy this." He smiled slightly.

His mother shrugged, then dropped her husband's hand and placed a hand in Xtina's.

Images flashed behind Xtina's eyes. She focused and decided on looking at the positive, instead of all the emotions boiling around inside her currently.

"When you were twelve, you were given a brand new pink Schwinn bike from your parents." She smiled at the memory. "You rode it everywhere and had a little custom license plate that had your name on it." The memories turned. "The first time you saw Rusty, you told your friend Rachelle that you were going to marry him."

Her hands dropped away from Xtina's as she gasped. "How did…?" Her words fell away, then she leaned closer. "How amazing."

The woman shocked Xtina by reaching out and taking her hands and turning them over as her eyes scanned them.

This time, Xtina let her mind wander over all the memories.

"You knew my parents." Her voice shook. "Kelly and Roy Warren."

Xtina watched Susan's eyes turn sad. "Yes, I'd heard they passed away."

"They were never right after…" Rusty broke in.

"After?" Mike asked, leaning his elbows on his knees.

His parents looked at one another.

"Can you see things?" Rusty asked. "If you…" He held out his hands.

Xtina hesitated for just one moment. Then she held out her hands and touched his. They were almost identical to Michael's, only slightly smaller and not as strong.

Her eyes closed as the images flooded her mind.

"Where you going, Rusty?" Her father, Roy, was younger than she'd ever seen him, either in her memories or in photos. His hair was longer than ever before, as well. Roy rushed over to a much younger Rusty and slapped him on the back. "We were going to have ourselves a party tonight."

"I don't know, my folks…"

"Won't find out. Come on." Her father nudged him. "Bring Sue. Kelly and Rachelle are coming. Larry is too."

She felt Rusty change his mind and figure out

how he was going to get out of going to the church services he was supposed to be attending that evening with his family.

Then the scene changed. The three couples were walking in the dark, carrying old flashlights as they sipped beer and laughed. Someone stumbled, and the entire group laughed.

The next moment was full of screams, running, and terror, so much so that Xtina almost dropped his hands.

But then everything settled down and it was the next day. Rusty sat in class, his hands on the desk as Roy walked over to him.

"Hey, man," Rusty said, trying to hide the fear.

Roy turned his nose up and walked away.

Then they flew to days later. Each time he tried to talk to Roy, he would shun him. He watched as Roy and Kelly stood in the hallway at school quietly whispering, then turning their backs away when friends walked by.

Rusty broke the connection.

"What happened?" she asked once all the memories had cleared from her mind. "What did you see that night? Where did you go?"

Sue reached over and took his hand. "Rusty?"

Just then there was a knock on the door, causing everyone to jump slightly. Mike glanced over at her, then frowned as he walked over to the door.

258

"Oh," Jessie said when she saw all the people in the living room. "I didn't know you had company. Xtina?"

"What is it?" Xtina stood up quickly. She noticed that her friend's face was paler than normal.

"I thought you would want to see…" Jessie held a newspaper out, her eyes moving around the room. "I came as fast as I could."

Xtina walked slowly over towards her friend, her eyes glued to the paper as her gut sank.

There, on the front cover of the county paper, was an image of her picking Rose up from the vet after her checkup. She glanced down at the dog now, who had been curled up by Mike's feet the entire time.

Her eyes turned back to the paper. Its headline read, "Local woman, believing herself to be psychic, thinks she's solved murder."

She allowed Mike to take the paper from her and he read the article out loud. She didn't really pay attention as Mike read the article detailing how Laura's husband had been murdered, and how Laura had been a victim herself when she'd shown up for their date night. It talked in detail of how she'd been jumped and had been knocked unconscious, then had been immediately accused by Christina Warren. They went on to describe her as a local woman who was visiting Hidden Creek after both of her parents were killed in a mysterious accident.

"Mysterious?" she piped in, not caring too much about the rest. "What do they mean..." She took the paper from Mike's hand and scanned the print until she found the part about her parents. "What do they mean by mysterious?" Her eyes moved to Mike's. "No one talked to me about this." She shook the paper. "The police chief said..." She felt her eyes tear up.

"Oh, honey." Susan was beside her, her arms around her shoulders before she could prepare herself.

The images that flooded her were that of pain so deep that she hunched over and cried out.

It was a week before Susan's seventeenth birthday. She should be at the lake with her friends. Instead, she was in a stale stark white room. Her legs were high above her head in stirrups and she was in more pain than she had ever been in her life. Her parents stood outside the glass, looking disapprovingly at her. Hours later, as the baby finally slid out of her, she cried out even though she was too tired to move and was covered in sweat.

She heard a cry, but then nothing as it was rushed from the room without her being able to even see it.

"I want..." she called out. "Nooo!" She tried to fight them. She wanted her baby.

"Shhh, it's okay. Your son will have a wonderful life," a nurse said, just before there was a slight prick and then darkness.

Xtina was jerked into reality by Mike's hands shaking her slightly. "Damn it, get some water," he called out.

Moments later, there was a glass put up to her lips and she drank, then coughed.

"Sorry, I though whiskey would be better," his father said.

It did the job more quickly than water normally did. "I'm fine." She coughed again. "Thanks." Her eyes watered as she looked up at Rusty. "No." She stopped the man from reaching down and helping her up. "Mike will…"

Mike pulled her up until she stood next to him. "She can't read me." He gave his mom a slight smile.

"Oh," Susan said, "honey, I'm so sorry."

"It's okay." She tried to smile. "I should have told you… about…" She shook her head and closed her eyes, almost a little embarrassed. Then she remembered the article. "What do they mean, mysterious?"

"I wanted to talk to you about… I did a little digging and if I felt there was something funny, it was only a matter of time before the police would find it too." He took her shoulders and led her to the sofa, then nudged until she sat down. Rose jumped up and snuggled next to her. Her hands dug into the dog's soft fur.

She waited until Mike walked over and downed a few fingers of the honey liquid his father had supplied. "Better?" Rusty asked her from his spot across the room.

"Yes, thank you." Her eyes moved back to Mike as everyone gained their seats again. She felt like her heart had refused to beat until he started speaking again.

***

Mike took a deep breath and started going over his findings. The lack of tire marks on the road, the angle that the car had taken the turn. From his experience as an investigator, he knew there was more to the story.

"Actually, I was going to go into the station and talk to Jacob about it later this week." His eyes moved to his parents.

"We'll go together." Xtina started to stand up.

"Now?" he asked, his eyes going again to his folks.

"I don't know if you finished reading that..." She glanced over at the paper. "But, in a roundabout way, I've just been accused of murdering my parents and accusing an innocent woman of murdering her husband. They're making me out to be..."

"Crazy," Jessie supplied, earning her a glare

from almost every eye in the room. "What?" she said, crossing her arms over her head. "It's not like I believe them. I've been her friend for longer than most…"

Xtina chuckled. "It's not the first time I've been called crazy. Nor will it be the last." She sighed and turned to Mike. "I'm going in to talk to Jacob about this tonight. If you don't want to come"—her eyes moved slightly to his parents— "I'll understand."

At that moment he didn't give a damn what his parents wanted. There was no way he was going to leave her alone in this.

"No, we'll all go." His father stood up and took his mother's hand. "It's high time we met our son."

They climbed into two different cars. Xtina insisted she ride with Jessie, who was still visibly upset about everything, while he drove his parents' car into town. He didn't trust his parents to drive in the dark in the emotional state they were in.

When he parked the car at the station, he helped his mother out just as Xtina and Jessie parked next to them.

When she got out of the car, there was a bright flash, which caused him to blink several times before he could respond. The next minute he was on the guy with the camera.

"Who the hell…" He had the guy by the jacket, his camera in the other hand.

ill Sanders

"Son," he heard his father calling to him, "it's not a crime to take pictures." Suddenly his mind cleared. His father was right. Quickly he dropped his hands and stepped back.

"I ought to sue you," the man said, straightening his jacket. Then his eyes moved to Xtina, who had moved closer to them. Her chin was held up high.

"Since you're taking pictures, how about a quote?" she said. He walked over and tugged on her arm.

"Let's go inside," he said under his breath.

"No, I'd like to have my say." Her eyes moved back to the cameraman.

"I don't take quotes, lady. Just pictures." He snapped a few more of her, then had the balls to turn his camera on him and snap off a few shots. He turned with a smile on his lips and walked away.

"Let's go inside," Xtina said softly as she took his hand. He was still vibrating with anger but knew there was nothing, legally, he could do at this point.

When they walked into the station, he stepped up to the desk clerk and asked if Jacob was on shift.

"He should be back"—the clerk looked at his watch— "'bout half an hour. You're welcome to wait unless there's something someone else can

264

help out with."

"No, we'll wait," Xtina said, then stepped back when the clerk's eyes grew big. Mike noticed the paper sitting on the desk and released a low growl of frustration.

"It's okay," Xtina said, squeezing his hand slightly. "News travels fast in small towns, but you add a local paper and…" She made a rocket sound and motion with her hand, then smiled at him. "Let's go have a seat." She tugged on his hand until he followed the group to the chairs across the room.

They ended up waiting only ten minutes before Jacob walked in, a young kid under his watchful eye. "Stay." He pointed to the kid and a chair. "Until I can call your folks."

The kid moved quickly and fell into the chair obediently.

When Jacob's eyes landed on the group, Mike noticed his eyes zero in on his parents.

"I can't do this now," Jacob said when he walked over to him.

"It's about my parents' accident," Xtina broke in, standing up.

Jacob's eyes moved to her and Mike noticed that they softened. Then they moved back over to him and rolled. "Give me a few minutes to call the kid's parents, then come on back."

They sat back down as Jacob disappeared down a hallway. The kid started to bolt towards the door, but when Michael cleared his throat loudly, he sat back down and looked at him in fear.

"What are you in for?" he asked the kid.

"Nothin." The kid tucked his hands into his pockets.

"Tagging isn't as much fun in a small town," he observed, tilting his head and nodding to the fresh spray paint on the kid's clothes.

"What would you know about it?" The kid jerked his chin up.

"Enough to know that you look like you'd be pretty talented at it." He crossed his arms over his chest and sized the kid up. "I've got a few things around my house that could use some paint. If you're interested in a job?" He glanced towards the front desk. "Might even get you out of some trouble with the folks."

"Yeah?" The kid leaned forward a little. "What kind of stuff?" Then his chin rose slightly. "What kind of pay we talking about?"

"An old garage. How about two dollars an hour? I'll supply all the paint."

"Can I do what I want?" he asked.

"Sure, I was thinking of something colorful. The only one who can see it is me."

The kid thought about it, then pulled out a piece

of paper from his pocket.

"How 'bout something like this?" He handed over the paper and Mike whistled when he saw the intricate drawing of flowers, bees, butterflies, and a large dragon in the middle.

"Like I said, you looked talented." He smiled. "That's just what I was looking for."

"Really?" Jacob walked back out and Mike handed the kid the paper again. He quickly tucked it back in his pocket.

"Looks like I've hired the kid to do some work out at my place," Mike supplied.

Jacob's eyes rolled. "Whatever." Then he turned to the kid. "Your folks are on their way. Sounds like you've already got your community service set up." He glanced at Mike.

"Be here early Saturday morning…"

"Damion," the kid supplied.

He jotted down his address. "Damion, if you let me keep the drawing, I'll make sure to have all the right colors ready for you. I'm Mike."

The kid handed the folded paper back to him. "Thanks, Mike." The kid's eyes lit up as they followed Jacob out of the room.

"That was a sweet thing you did," Xtina said, following him out of the room. He reached down and took her hand.

He didn't know if she knew it yet or not, but the look in her eyes told him that she loved him more than any words ever could.

Chapter Eighteen

Xtina tried to hide her anxiety. She didn't like being in such a small room with so many people. Especially people who were so full of emotions at the moment.

There was enough anxiety in the room to send her own over the edge. She had to focus on controlling things. Mike was like her rock, keeping her grounded, which helped more than she would have ever guessed.

When the door shut behind him, Jacob turned around. "I assume you're Susan and Rusty Kincaid?"

Rusty's arms were wrapped around his wife.

"Jacob, these are my parents," Mike broke in.

"Our parents."

Jacob held up a finger. "First, I know why you're here." He turned to Xtina. "I saw the article, and I can assure you, we are not looking at you as a suspect in the investigation into your parents' accident."

"The fact that there is an investigation into my parents' death is why I'm here." She continued to hold on to Mike's hand, but raised her chin slightly to get her point across. "Why didn't you mention any of this last night?"

Jacob's eyes moved to Mike's. "You know how this works. You used to be on the force."

Mike nodded. "Honey, they can't talk to you because it's an ongoing investigation."

She dropped his hand and turned on him. "I didn't expect him to give me all the details, just tell me they *had* an ongoing investigation," she almost growled out.

"I didn't know myself until this morning," Jacob broke in. "Dan told me."

"Dan?" she asked, keeping her arms crossed over her chest.

"Yeah, he's lead investigator in the case." He rubbed his forehead as if he had a headache.

"Well, can I talk to him?" she asked.

"No. Not about the case. Not unless he has questions for you or he has found something."

271

She took a slow breath, then released it. "Well, the fact that someone talked to the local paper about the case and hinted that I *was* a suspect..."

"Trust me," he said, "I have every intention of finding out who leaked the story," Jacob said. Then his eyes turned to the couple standing in the room, still holding one another, and she felt instant shame.

Here they were, together as a family for the first time, and she was too focused on herself to allow them time alone.

"Well, I guess that will have to do for now." She reached over and took Jessie's hand and tugged on it. "Jess, why don't we step out for a soda." She winked at Mike before shutting the door behind them.

"What was that for?" Jess asked once they were in the hallway by themselves.

"I figured they needed some time alone," she answered as she walked towards the soda machines at the end of the hallway.

"Why?" Jess followed closely.

She stopped when she realized Jessie had no clue that the two men were brothers. "Because..." She wondered briefly if she should be the one to tell her, then realized it was Jessie she was talking to, her best friend... her only friend. "Jacob is their son," she said softly.

"What?" Jessie almost yelled it.

"Shh." She tugged on Jessie's hand until they stepped into a dark room near the soda machines. Xtina's eyes darted around to make sure they were alone.

"Jacob? Jacob St. Clair is Michael's brother?" she whispered.

"Yes." It was her turn to rub her forehead. "His parents had him when they were young and gave him up for adoption and here we are."

Jessie shook her head, her eyes glued to the doorway at the end of the hallway where the family was having their first meeting. "I…"

"What is it between you and Jacob?" Xtina crossed her arms over her chest.

"Nothing," Jessie answered too quickly, making Xtina just glare at her. "Fine, he arrested me." She rolled her eyes.

"What?" This time it was Xtina's turn to be shushed. "What happened?"

"I locked myself out of my apartment one night and decided to try and break in through the back window. How was I to know jumping the fence was breaking and entering old man Wilson's backyard. Either way, after a night in the cell, everything smoothed itself out. But Jacob knew who I was and where I lived, yet he still hauled me in. He's just a mean jerk." She could see the heat and anger behind her friend's eyes.

"He was just doing his job," she assured Jessie.

273

"Yeah." They both jumped when the door at the end of the hallway slammed open and Jacob walked out, his face skewed with anger.

His eyes zeroed in on her as he walked by. "I don't give a damn if they are my folks, I don't want to see them back here."

She nodded. "Sorry," she said softly. He nodded, then disappeared after glaring briefly at Jessie.

"Told ya," Jessie said under her breath.

Xtina rode with Mike and his parents back to his place in silence. She picked up Rose, who had found a perfect place to sleep on Mike's pillow, and started walking home.

"Hey," Mike said, catching up with her when she was halfway home. She stopped and turned to him. "Were you trying to sneak out without saying goodbye?"

"Sorry." Her eyes moved to his house. Every light was on and she could hear his parents talking and his mother crying. "I thought they might like some time…"

Mike glanced back and nodded. "Yeah." He rolled his eyes. "Needless to say, it didn't go well."

"I'm sorry."

He took her hands in his and shook his head. "Don't be. My parents understand. They're just happy they have finally found their lost son. Not to mention the pressure of keeping a secret is off their chests."

She thought about all the secrets she was holding in. It would be nice not having the weight of them on her.

"I understand." His finger brushed her chin, tipping it up lightly until their eyes met in the darkness. "Mike, I…" She closed her eyes, but felt him stiffen when the dog started to growl softly.

Her eyes flew open as Rose took off across the yard, towards her house.

"Did you leave those lights on?" Mike asked, his hand tightening in hers.

"N… no. Just the porch light."

"Stay put," Mike called back to her after taking off towards her house himself.

"Wait," she called out to him, following him.

"Xtina! I mean it," he said in a hushed tone. "Stay. Better yet, go get my dad. Tell him my gun is in the safe, with my birthday as the code."

She stopped, then glanced back at his house. When she looked back at Mike, he had disappeared completely in the darkness.

Fear immediately spiked through her. She wanted to rush after him, but common sense won out. They needed help.

She was out of breath by the time she burst in the front door. His parents were huddled together on the sofa; the tears were almost dry on his mother's face.

"What?" Rusty stood quickly.

"Someone... Someone's in my house. Mike needs his gun." She rushed on. "His bedroom closet, the code is his—"

"Birthday," his father called out as he rushed to the back of the room.

"Oh dear." His mother gripped the pillow. "Should we call the police?"

"Not yet," Rusty said as he rushed out. "It might not be anything." He tossed his cell phone over to his wife. "Wait on the porch, we'll call out if we need anything."

Before she could respond, he was gone. Susan followed her out onto the front porch where they stood together, waiting. Xtina's nails dug into the wood railing as the silence echoed in her mind.

She couldn't even hear Rose barking anymore. Worry dominated her entire body.

She tried to shoot her powers towards her room, but couldn't feel anything.

She thought about the night she'd sensed Laura, and knew that it had been because she'd been with Mike that her powers had extended. She glanced over at Mike's mother.

"I want to try something, if you're up to it?" She held out her hand, and waited.

"Are you sure?" Susan asked.

Xtina nodded.

When Susan touched her, power shot through her entire body. Focusing, she shot her mind across the tall grass, towards her house.

"Mike's searching my bedroom. Rusty's searching the downstairs." Her mind spread out across the house. "No one else is there." She took a deep breath, then felt it and stiffened. "Someone was." She shivered at the message he'd left on her bathroom mirror for only her eyes to see.

She dropped Susan's hand and started walking towards her house.

"Honey? Are you okay?" Susan asked, catching up with her.

"Yes," she said dryly. "It's okay. It was just an old friend." She tried to smile for the woman. "I'll have them come back. Thank you for the wonderful dinner. I'm sorry about… Jacob."

"It's okay." Susan patted her hand, then dropped her arm beside her. "He'll come around, once things have calmed down."

"Yes, he just needs time." She smiled. "Goodnight." She marched towards her house and called out to the men.

"It's clear," she called out. Rusty met her first.

"You sure?" he asked.

She nodded to where Rose lay in her bed, fast asleep. "Yup." She smiled. "I think Susan needs you tonight. Thank you." She leaned up and placed a kiss on his cheek. "Goodnight."

He nodded, then left.

"Everything okay?" Mike asked from the base of the stairs. She turned slowly as Rusty shut the front door softly behind him.

She couldn't hold back the emotions any longer, so she decided not to. Without saying a word, she moved across the empty space and took his face in her hands and pressed her lips and body against his. She poured everything she had into the kiss. Every ounce of love she'd ever dreamed of having, she showed him now, knowing that she would never have it again.

Her body reacted to his instantly. She backed him up the stairs slowly, but his hands moved quickly over hers, pulling, tugging her sweater dress up, over her skin. He reversed their positons and she lay on the top stair, her legs spread wide as his body crushed her to the upstairs landing.

His mouth moved quickly over her, heating her until she felt every ounce of love back from him. She heard fabric rip as she tugged his shirt over his head, yanked at his jeans until they slid down his hips. Then her legs wrapped around his hips, holding him to her, taking her quickly. Speed. It was all she needed. To love him quickly as she took him into her, faster, until she cried out and heard him follow.

***

"My god!" he grunted as he looked down at Xtina. Her dark hair was fanned out on the carpet. Her legs had fallen from around his hips and were laying down the stairs.

His knees would have bruises where the stair had jammed into them as he'd pumped into her. He felt himself grow hard just thinking about it again.

"My god!" he said again and shook the image from his mind. He needed a moment to catch his breath. To think. He closed his eyes at her beautiful green eyes staring back up at him. When his eyes opened again, he smiled slightly. "Tell me that didn't mean… what it meant."

He watched her green eyes slide closed. "Mike…"

He growled, then pushed up from the floor, taking her with him. "Don't give me that shit," he said next to her ear. He was pissed now. Hell, he was tired of her hiding herself from him.

He moved until her shoulders were pushed up against the wall, her naked body tight against his.

"Feel this?" He gripped her hand to his heart. "It beats for you. For this." He pushed inside her again and watched as those eyes turned foggy once again. "Feel it match your heartbeat?" He pumped his hips and had her moaning with pleasure. "Take it all," he growled next to her ear, then he nipped at

279

her with his teeth. "Everything is yours." He felt himself slip even more into her soul. "It's empty without you." He knew he was being rough when he took her hands and yanked them above her head, holding her there. Their eyes locked. "Tell me."

She shook her head slightly, causing him to push her even harder, faster. "Xtina," he warned, "you can't hide it from me." He watched her eyes soften as her hand broke free and reached for his face. When she brushed a finger down his chin, he knew he'd won. "Say it," he repeated.

"I…" She sighed and he felt her tense around him. "I love you," she cried out as her eyes closed.

He carried her into the bedroom and fell on the comforter, but after that, he must have clocked out for a few hours. When he woke, it was to screams. He jerked himself up, wide-awake and staring at his ghost. Non-ghost.

Feeling around, he realized the bed was empty and cold next to him.

"Damn." He ran a hand over his face, then jerked to attention. "What are you doing here?" It still got him. Seeing her outside his house.

The dark eyes stared back at him as the mouth opened widely and closed. One of her hands rose and pointed out the window.

He could hear Rose barking in the background. "Xtina?" His eyes moved around the room.

He heard it again, a scream, and jerked up, grabbing his pants and the gun he'd left in her nightstand. He threw on his shoes and grabbed the coat hanging by the back door.

"Xtina?" He continued to call out as he ran in the direction from which he'd heard Rose. There was a light rain falling and every now and then a flash of lightning would light up the dark sky.

Reaching into the pocket, he was happy to find the flashlight she'd put there the night they'd found Rose.

"Rose?" he called out when a sudden silence cut the night. He stopped and listened but could only hear his heavy breathing. "Rose?" he called out softly, listening. Nothing. Not even a whimper.

His mind snapped to Xtina. Why would she come out here? His mind was working for the first time. She wouldn't. Someone had been in the house earlier. Someone she'd known and been afraid of.

He thought back to how she'd reacted when she'd come in. Had she fallen asleep next to him when he'd carried her upstairs to the bed? Or had she waited for…

He closed his eyes. If there was any ounce of power in him, he called to it now. He felt an urgency to find her, but nothing more.

Slowly he took deep breaths and tried to focus on thinking about only her. He felt a slow buzz travel up his legs, through his arms, and settle over his heart. He felt a pulse, then opened his eyes and somehow knew the direction to run.

His mind called to her, screamed for her as he felt pain shoot through his entire body, knowing that it was her pain he was feeling.

Feel me, he called out to her mind. *I'm coming. Fight it. Fight for me.*

Chapter Nineteen

*X*tina tried to fight. She'd known they'd been there but hadn't thought they would return so soon. She'd fallen asleep in Mike's arms and then had woken when arms tightened around her. A hand had covered her mouth as she'd felt a prick in her neck.

The drugs had caused her entire body to lock up, her eyes frozen open. She'd tried to kick and fight, but couldn't move. A white cloak had been wrapped around her naked body and she'd been carried out of the house.

Her face was covered as her body was carried for what seemed like hours.

She remained paralyzed until the cold blade of a

sharp knife pressed against her breast. Her body jerked slightly at the feeling of the metal against her bare skin.

"Our mother has returned," the voice she'd come to dread spoke above her. Her eyes refused to focus but she could see the outline of William Ray hovering above her as his knife slid slowly across her bare chest. The dribble of blood shone in the firelight. She glanced around and couldn't feel her power at all. The drugs. The same ones they had used to bind her last time, in Arizona.

"Mike," she cried out, trying to send what she had to him. She screamed when the blade slid once more across her skin and more blood oozed out of her.

"Our mother has returned to show us the way," William cried out. She could hear several other of his close followers chanting the same thing over and over again in Latin.

She knew the message well. "Mother oh Mother, show us what is to be done."

She wasn't a seer or an oracle, but these people didn't care. Once William had found out about her powers, he'd changed from a loving boyfriend to the money- and power-hungry person he was now. He had made it very clear that he would do *anything* to gain her power. She had the scars to prove it.

She cried out again when he leaned down and

drew her bloody breast into his mouth and sucked the red liquid into his mouth. When he leaned up again, his face was covered in her blood and she screamed again. She'd escaped this crazy before, but now... Her mind cried again for Mike.

At one point, in her fogginess, she had imagined she'd heard Rose, but now all was quiet.

Her eyes opened and she watched his dark eyes scanning his audience.

"This is just the beginning," he continued, his preaching voice ringing out, vibrating back to him. It was then that she looked around and realized where they were. "We shall take our mother back with us and begin a new chapter. One where our children will be seekers of the truth. With this power, we shall be ready for what is to come."

Cheers erupted, causing more echoes to vibrate through the hidden bunker.

"Billy." She coughed, trying to clear the drugs from her body. "Don't do this."

His dark eyes moved down to hers. "You should have never left," he hissed next to her ear. "I told you, you're mine and always will be." His hand covered her breast and she felt bile roll in her stomach. "You'll be the mother to my children, children who will usher this world to the next." He smiled, showing off the perfect teeth she'd actually enjoyed looking at once.

She'd been so young and naive when she'd fallen for the leader of the Humanist Society. It hadn't bothered her that he'd been almost ten years her senior or that he'd been married twice before. She'd been so busy looking for an escape from her parents' crazy religious hold that she'd fallen right into a crazier one.

"You can't do this." She tried to think of a way out of it. She silently sent all her energy once more towards Michael. Please, she begged in her mind, find me.

"We have to move quickly," William said, his hands going up to quiet the group. "Everything is ready; we've prepared for this. You each know what needs to be done." She heard most of the small group of people start to leave the room.

She felt her body being lifted. She was still unable to move due to the drugs in her system, and she wondered how long it would be before they started dosing her regularly like they had last time.

"Please," she cried out. "Water." It was a stall tactic, but it had always worked before. They wanted her contained but alive and well.

She was laid back down, while a bottle of liquid was produced. She knew it would be clean, void of any chemicals, as would any food they would feed her. The only foreign substance allowed in her body now was the mixture of natural herbs and roots that kept her under their power.

The water helped release some of the hold the drugs had on her and she shot what was remaining of her power towards Mike. She didn't know if she was doing any good.

She continued to swallow the water, then felt something deep inside shift. Her mind opened and she felt someone else, someone new. Like white lights turning on in the darkness, her mind cleared.

She called out to each one, screaming for help, showing them the room she was in, the red metal door, the number of people she'd seen, William.

She heard the door shut behind the last follower and realized she was now alone with William once more. Knowing what it meant, she started to fight, but this time when the needle slipped into her skin, she knew, without a doubt, that they would come to save her. The power was too great for them to ignore or deny. Something greater than her had been awakened.

***

Mike stood in the field and watched a group of heavily armed people move around, loading a dark van of supplies.

He wondered if they had been there that day he'd searched the place. He'd scoured the place from top to bottom. How had he missed them?

He was squatting behind a tree when the images flashed quickly behind his eyes, almost knocking him on his ass.

Red door, seven people, Xtina screaming for help.

He held on to the trunk of the tree to steady himself. What the hell? He shook his head and watched as two men pulled the van closer to the door.

He'd searched everywhere, except that first red metal door, which had been locked. The same door that Xtina had convulsed outside of.

At his count, there were six of them, which meant only one was still inside. The group continued to load up the van slowly, hindered only by the darkness of the night, since they weren't using flashlights.

His mind snapped to the cover over the silo and sent a silent prayer that there wasn't someone guarding it. He moved to the open field, staying as low as he could. He'd just found the opening, when he heard footsteps behind him.

"Well," Jacob said, rushing up behind him, "are you going to stand here all night or are we going to do this?" The man was wearing black sweat pants and a sweatshirt, like he'd just climbed out of bed and thrown on the first thing that he'd found.

Mike was thankful that he had his gun strapped to his waist. "How…?" he started to ask.

"You felt it, too," his brother said quickly, then knelt at the small opening of the silo. "Damn." He looked up at him. "Do you think you can squeeze through?"

Mike set his gun and flashlight down, then

tried, putting his legs in first. "The ladder should be…" He felt the top rung with his foot. "Got it." He smiled. "Hand me my gun when I'm down." Jacob nodded, then held on to his hands as he helped him wiggle through the opening. "Then get help." He looked up into his brother's eyes.

"Already done. I called it in before coming here myself."

Mike nodded and moved until his shoulders cleared the heavy door. When his fingers wrapped around the top rung, he released a breath. "I'm in." He held his hand out and took his weapon. He tucked it in his back pocket and took the flashlight Jacob held out for him.

Jacob called, "I'm coming in after you."

Mike quickly made it down the rungs, then watched as Jacob came in, much like he had.

When they both reached the bottom, both of their feet were soaked.

"This way," he called out as he made his way towards the staircase. He could hear Jacob following him. They made their way up the stairs, down the maze of tunnels until he stopped just at the long end of the last hallway.

"Down there, they have to be at the end of this one, off to the right, there's a…"

"Red metal door," Jacob stated, which had Mike glancing at him.

"Yeah." He turned back to scan the darkness.

"Later, we're going to have to have a talk."

"Yeah." Jacob pulled out his weapon. "Lead the way."

Mike pushed off, listening for any sounds, but heard nothing.

When they turned the last corner, he flipped off his flashlight and the darkness was almost blinding. Soon, though, he could see the flicker of candlelight coming from under the red door.

"We have one chance at this," he said, then he heard voices above and knew that the police were battling their own fight upstairs.

Jacob glanced up and Mike could see the worry flash behind his eyes. "Go. By my count, there's only one left in here with Xtina."

Jacob didn't hesitate, but took off up the stairs at a quick pace.

Mike hoped that the metal door had muffled some of the noises from above, so that when he opened it, he wouldn't be walking into a trap.

When he kicked open the door, he was disappointed when a spray of bullets hit around him and pain shot out in several places on his body.

His left side was on fire, as was his upper thigh, causing him to duck quickly behind the thick cement wall.

"You're surrounded," he called out as he pulled

the rest of his body from the opening.

"There can only be one ending," a man's voice called out. "One in which our mother is returned to us." More bullets struck the hallway and bounced off the metal door or imbedded themselves in the cement walls. "She's mine. She is a part of me. She's my bride, the mother to my children,"

Later, Mike thought, he would have to find out what that meant, but for now, all he wanted was to know if Xtina was safe.

"If you've hurt her," he called out.

"I would never!" More shots shouted out.

Just then Mike's phone chimed and he glanced down. It was the alarm he'd set to mark when his nightly visitor would be arriving. He leaned his head back against the cold cement wall and thought of how his life had taken such a drastic turn since that first night over a year ago when he'd first been woken up by his ghost.

"What the…" More shots sounded, followed by a loud scream. "Go away!" He heard the gun cock, but then heard the telltale sounds of an empty chamber as the man continued to pull the trigger repeatedly.

Mike didn't hesitate. He rolled into the doorway, his gun drawn before him.

He didn't have to search the dark room for the man, since his ghost was hovering directly in front of him, hovering over Xtina's naked body as she lay on a large wood table.

Aiming his gun, Mike watched as the man started reloading his gun. Without hesitating, Mike fired off two shots, straight through the man's heart.

He fell backwards, a shocked look in his eyes. He'd seen that look before, on his partner's face so many years ago. He felt every muscle in his body relax, knowing the man wouldn't be getting up again.

He watched as the misty figure turned to him, her dark eyes turning soft as she glanced down at him. Then, with a slight smile, she disappeared into thin air.

It was then that the pain surfaced. He groaned as he rolled over and jumped to his feet. When he reached Xtina's side, he wrapped the white cloak around her body, taking stock of the small cuts along her bare skin. They weren't deep enough to need stitches, and he figured they could be dealt with after he got her outside.

Her eyes were locked in the open position, giving him quite a scare, but he could feel a pulse and her chest rose and fell with steady breaths.

"You're okay," he assured her. "I'm here." He leaned down and placed a kiss on her lips as tears slid down his face and fell onto hers.

She blinked, then he felt her arms wrap around his shoulders.

"Mike." His name came out as a whisper.

"I'm here," he cried out. "It's over." He lifted her gently, feeling the pain shoot through his leg and side, but ignoring them.

"Mike," she said again, her arms falling from his shoulders.

"Shh, I've got you." He paused outside the door and listened above. The night had grown silent and he wondered suddenly if Jacob was okay.

"It's all clear up here," someone called out. "We're sending help down to you."

"No," he called out, "we're coming up." He doubted he would be able to make it up the flights of stairs himself, but he wanted to no matter what.

"Mike," she cried out, until he looked down at her.

"What?" He brushed a kiss across her lips. "We'll be out of here soon."

"No." She shook her head slightly. "I... I can't hold it back any more."

"What?" He shifted her so he could bring her closer to him.

"My love for you," she said softly as tears streamed down her face. "I know I'm not supposed to have a happy ever after, it wasn't in my cards, but…"

He shook his head. "That's just plain silly. Everyone deserves happiness."

"No, not me. I'm… different." Her arms once more came around him as he started climbing the stairs slowly. "It was always going to end in tragedy."

He pulled her close. "Tonight didn't. We're safe."

She closed her eyes as he made the last turn and started the final set of stairs. His leg was starting to go numb, but he knew it was his task alone to bring her out of the darkness.

"Mike." She brushed a hand along the side of his face. "I can't deny it any longer. No matter what happens, I don't care anymore. Whatever comes, know that I will always love you."

He stopped at the top of the stairs, the fresh air hitting them both from the open door. His breathing was labored and he was pretty sure he was on the verge of passing out, but he wanted to hold on to the moment and stepped out into the cold winter night.

"Xtina, I've loved you from the moment I laid eyes on you. Even before we met. I would do anything to protect you. To ensure that you have a long, healthy, happy life… with me." He smiled as Jacob rushed over to him. He leaned down and brushed a kiss across her lips before he felt himself spinning out of control and fading off into the darkness he'd been fighting off.

Chapter Twenty

Xtina felt herself falling and cried out, but then she was lifted and caught with strong arms.

"Easy," Jacob's voice called out. "Someone help. I've got you."

"Mike?" she asked, wishing her body would respond to her commands. Instead, she lay in Jacob's arms, useless.

"He's out. Help is on the way." She felt him shift and then lay her down gently. "Here," he called out.

Rose rushed over and started covering her face with kisses. Jacob pulled the dog away gently. "Easy, she's okay," he reassured the dog as someone pulled her back.

Xtina turned her head and watched as Jacob worked on Mike. His hands came away covered in blood, causing her to finally be able to move in fear.

She turned over and reached out for Mike's hand, a few inches from her own. When their hands touched, power flowed between them and she closed her eyes, willing every last ounce of energy into him to allow him to fight.

When she woke next, she was in a soft bed, warm and safe.

"There you are," Jessie said, leaning over her, looking down at her. "You scared the shit out of me." Her friend sat next to her and brushed a strand of hair away from her eyes.

"Sorry," she said. Her throat burned slightly. Then it all came back to her. "Mike?" She tried to sit up.

"Easy." Jess held her down. "He's in surgery. They're pulling the bullet out of his leg."

"How…" She started to say, then ended up having a coughing fit.

"Here, drink some water." Jess held up a glass with a straw. She sucked up the liquid and sighed when it cooled her throat.

"How is he?" she asked after a moment.

"I'm not sure. His folks wanted to see you, if you're up for it?"

Xtina nodded slightly. She shifted, noticing for the first time that she had bandages over the cuts on her skin. She wrapped the hospital gown tighter around her and pulled the blankets up as Jessie piled another pillow behind her head.

"Thanks," she said before taking another sip of water.

"I saw it, you know." Jess sat down again next to her. "The message." She closed her eyes. "The red door, the seven people, the pain." Tears fell from her friend's face and dropped on their joined hands.

"I'm… sorry." She shook her head.

"No, don't be. I know you sent them. I didn't understand, but I came, when you called." She smiled, then laughed. "Talk about some crazy shit."

Xtina chuckled, then held still when pain shot out from her ribs.

"Oh yeah, the doctor said you have a bruised rib or two."

"Thanks for the warning." She moaned and held her chest.

"Sorry." Jessie stood up. "We'll talk later, when we're all together."

"Who?" she asked, feeling her energy fade.

Jess shook her head. "You won't believe me if I tell you anyway." She walked towards the door.

"Let's just say, you're more powerful than even you knew." She turned to go, then turned back to her. "Don't scare me like that again," she warned, then she smiled and walked out.

She felt her mind turning over with worry about Mike, but waited until his folks walked in. Susan's face was pale, but she had a smile on.

"Hi," they both said in unison. "You doing okay?"

Xtina sat up a little more, holding her chest.

"Yes, any word on Mike?"

"The bullet just grazed his side, but the one in his leg," Rusty said, glancing over at Susan.

"They're working on taking it out. It lodged in his muscle." She sighed. "He'll be fine."

A doctor walked in and smiled at them. "I was told I could find you in here." He glanced over at her. "How are you feeling?"

"Fine. Mike?" she asked, feeling her pulse kick in.

"He's out of surgery." He smiled. "Came out like a trooper. Good thing it hadn't gone in far. He should be good enough to be released in a few days."

She relaxed back and heard both of his parents release sighs of relief.

"We'll let you get some rest." Susan walked

over and patted her hand. "Is there someone else you wish us to call?"

"No. I have my family here." She smiled up at them. "Thanks. Keep me posted."

"We have Rose," Rusty broke in before they left. "She'll stay with us until you can go home."

"Thanks. Is she okay?"

"Yes, just shaken up a little," Susan said.

Then she turned to the doctor. "Can I see him soon?"

"Well, I want to keep you overnight, but there shouldn't be too much trouble moving you into his room, once he's been moved out of post-op for the night. That is if it's okay with his parents?"

"Yes, of course," Rusty said with a smile. "I think he'd like that."

Less than two hours later, she fell asleep, listening to Mike's heart monitor beep next to her. She'd been wheeled into his room in a bed, but had crawled out of it and sat next to him on his bed. When she got tired, she sprawled next to his good side, making sure not to jostle him.

She woke when the nurses came in to check on him, then again in the morning when his arms wrapped around her shoulders.

"Hey," he moaned, trying to move.

She held him still. "Easy," she said, holding him close.

"I'm okay," he said softly into her hair.

"Yeah, so they keep telling me." She smiled up at him and noticed that his eyes weren't quite focused yet. "You're in pain?"

"It's better than being out. I'm okay."

"Sure you are." She reached for the button to call the nurse, but he stopped her.

"No, give me a moment to be with you." His arm tightened slightly, causing her to relax into his warmth.

She listened to his heartbeat and closed her eyes.

"Did you mean it?" he asked after a moment. She'd believed he'd gone back under, but now she leaned up and looked down at him.

"What?" she asked, her eyes moving over every inch of his face, wanting to remember everything about him.

"What you said, last night."

She smiled. "Yes, every word." She felt her heart swell.

"Tell me again." He brushed a strand of her hair away from her face. She knew it was probably a knotted mess, but didn't care.

"I love you." She felt her breath hitch. "I know I'm not supposed to..."

"Stop." He put a finger lightly over her lips.

"You're allowed to do whatever you want in life. We make our own paths." His eyes met hers. "After Cameron, I didn't think I would be able to trust again. Except for my family. Then you came along." His hand cupped her face and she enjoyed the warmth of it. "You shook things up, made me look at life from a different angle." He chuckled, then groaned. "A really different angle."

She smiled, worry flooding her. His speech was slurred and she could see that he was using up too much energy.

"Rest," she encouraged.

"Later, I'm not done." His eyes refocused. "You made me see things, feel things I didn't know I could. Or even that I wanted in my life. You filled an empty spot, one that I don't want empty anymore."

There was a knock on the door and a nurse walked in. "Good, you're awake. You have a visitor, if you're up for it?"

He shifted slightly. "Fine." He glanced back at her. "But this isn't over." He smiled. "Now, kiss me before…"

It was too late, Jacob walked in and coughed. "Sorry, I can come back later?"

"No," Mike said, tugging Xtina down for that kiss anyway.

"I think I'm going to go freshen up." She dreaded looking at herself in the mirror; she desperately wanted a shower.

"Jessie wanted me to give you this." He held up a bag. "She's getting you some food and should be up soon."

She took the bag, sending up a silent thank you to her friend, then disappeared into the bathroom.

When she peeled the hospital gown from her, she ran her eyes over every inch of her body. Her hair was a rat's nest, but Jessie had included a bottle of her favorite conditioner and she knew that would soon be resolved.

Her eyes ran lower. Bruises covered her ribs, arms, and legs, like she'd been dragged behind a truck. She even found pebbles in her knees and spent some time picking them out before climbing into the shower.

The hot water hit her and the emotions she'd been holding back spewed free, causing her knees to buckle.

Her mind raced over how close she'd come to losing everything. Mike, herself. Everything. Even before she'd ever really enjoyed life.

She sat on the cold tile floor and let everything out as the hot water cleaned her.

***

"You might as well sit down and spill it," Mike said, shifting. He held his breath against the pain, but focused on Jacob's face. He could tell there was a wall of shit heading his way and no amount of bracing for it would ease the pain of hearing what was coming next.

"Well." Jacob sat and leaned his elbows on his knees. "Looks like the group was a branch of the Humanist Society out of Arizona." He pulled out a folder that had been tucked under his arm. "We've got four of them in custody. Three of them, including William Ray, were killed last night in the fight."

"And?" He had figured this much already, the part about the Humanist Society being behind it. He'd recognized William Ray right away last night.

"Well, several of them are talking about what they had done to get Xtina back in town." He shook his head and ran his hand over his face. For the first time, Mike realized that Jacob looked like he hadn't gotten any sleep yet. "Well, they're hinting that they had something to do with her parents' deaths. Mind you"—his eyes met his own— "no one has confessed yet, but they were pretty sure Ray was behind the accident."

"How… How long had they been here?"

"It appears only a few days. They were setting up a more permanent place less than twenty miles from here." He looked down at the notes. "They were going to take 'their mother'—Xtina—to the location and start a new branch of the society with her as their mother." He threw down the folder.

"Christ almighty." He shook his head. "Talk about crazy."

Mike chuckled and then instantly regretted the move when his side started burning.

"You doing okay?" Jacob leaned forward, concern flooding his face.

"Yeah." He shook his head. "Guess I could go for some more meds." He reached for the button to call the nurse, but Jacob beat him to it.

"Thanks." He waited. "I mean it. For last night... for everything."

This time it was Jacob who laughed. "When you're feeling better, we're going to have a talk about the other kind of crazy shit that went down last night."

He nodded, just as a nurse walked in. "Later," he promised, then Jessie walked in, carrying a bag of fast food.

He almost laughed when she skirted around Jacob with a frown.

"Hey." She smiled at him. "Is Xtina in the shower?"

He nodded, already feeling the medicine flooding in his veins.

"Is it okay if I stay and wait for her to come out?" Jessie asked, her eyes moving to Jacob.

"Sure," he said, his speech already slurring. "Be

nice to my brother," he said before clocking out.

When he woke, Jessie and Xtina were sitting across the room, talking in low tones.

"Hey," he said, clearing his throat.

They both rushed over to him. "How are you feeling?" Xtina asked.

"Much better." He realized he was feeling pretty good.

"Your parents are back. They went and got some sleep last night."

"Good." He pulled her hand up to his lips and kissed her. "There are some things we have to talk about."

"I'll go get them." Jessie started to leave.

"Make sure you come back. You'll want to hear this too," he said.

When everyone was crowded into the small room, he glanced around. Xtina looked back to her normal self, albeit still a little pale. She'd changed into a thick pair of black leggings with a long purple and gray sweater over it. She'd tied her hair up into a long braid that flowed over her shoulder. She'd even applied some makeup, probably to hide the circles under her eyes and the bruises he could see hiding underneath.

He pulled her closer to his good side before opening his mouth to start relaying the information Jacob had given him earlier that day. His parents and Xtina listened patiently while he talked. Jessie, however, interrupted occasionally with questions, most of which he didn't have the answers to.

"When are they going to let me go home?" he asked after he was finished and the room remained silent.

"If they can get you up and walking with those"—Xtina nodded to the crutches leaning against the wall— "sometime tomorrow."

He nodded, then started to toss the sheets aside.

"No." She shook her head. "Food first." She stopped him from standing. "Take it slow, there's no hurry."

He relented when he felt his stomach growl. "Okay." He moved his good leg back onto the bed.

The rest of the day was filled with everyone coming and going. Several times his parents and Jessie left to grab food or run errands, but Xtina stayed by his side, only leaving to use the restroom or to get him some more water.

That evening, after saying goodnight to his parents, Xtina crawled into bed beside him and flipped through the channels on the TV. She quickly rushed by the news station, but he stopped her and took the remote.

After watching the reports on the local news, he realized why she'd been trying to keep the news from him. Once again, they were painting her as some sort of crazy involved in a cult instead of a

307

victim who had been snatched from her own bedroom.

"It's okay, really." She leaned back against his shoulder. "Jacob has assured me that when they make their official statement in the morning, everything will be cleared up."

"Why the hell is he waiting?"

"They're too close to getting a confession. He thinks by morning they will have at least one, if not all four."

All the fight left him as his arms wrapped around her. "Well, I guess we'll just have to wait then."

Once again, he drifted off to sleep, holding Xtina in his arms.

When he woke this time, his bed was empty and the room was still dark. He sat up, rubbed his hands across his face, and pushed his good leg over the edge of the bed with the idea of making it to the restroom on his own.

But instead of the cold hospital floor, he met only open air as he was tossed up in the air violently. Loud sounds crashed around him. Dust, rocks, dirt, and debris flew around him as bombs exploded a few yards away. His entire body shook violently as a searing pain shot from his arm and shoulder. When he looked down, he saw bone sticking out of his own flesh and felt blood trickling down his side. He must have screamed, because suddenly, Xtina's voice was calling out his name.

He woke with a start, the cold hospital floor underneath him, while Xtina stood over him.

"Ethan!" he cried out, trying to get to his feet.

"Easy!" She rushed to him. "I saw it too." She wrapped her arms around him. "He's okay." She told him over and over. "He's out."

He closed his eyes and prayed it was true.

"My folks," he said after a moment. She'd helped him back up onto the bed and had checked that the fall from the bed hadn't done any damage.

"I'll call them." She reached for his phone, just as it rang.

"It's Jacob," she said and then handed him the phone.

"Want to tell me what the hell just happened?" Jacob sounded angry. "What the hell did I just see?"

"What?" His eyes moved to Xtina's.

"Did you just get blown up or what?" Jacob finally asked.

"No, but I think our brother, Ethan, my twin, is in serious trouble." He closed his eyes as the images flashed once more in his mind.

Epilogue

Xtina sat across the room from Jessie and Jacob. Mike's parents had left moments ago, after relaying the call they had gotten less than two hours earlier. They had all crowded into her living room, while a fire heated up the entire house.

She was still a little shocked to learn that her parents had been murdered by William Ray, her ex-boyfriend. He had always claimed to be her husband, even though he'd drugged her and wed her himself, shortly before she'd escaped his clutches the first time.

Her eyes moved over to where Mike was propped up on the sofa. Rose snuggled by one of his feet as his bad leg was piled high on top of pillows.

Life had defiantly taken a turn for the better since she'd returned home.

After seeing Ethan being hurt, so much more had become clear to her. She was anxious to tell everyone, but the news about Mike's brother had outweighed her other news. She had sat back silently as his family worried, even though she now knew everything would turn out.

Mike's father had explained that they had received a call from Ethan's commanding officer.

If everything went smoothly, they'd be shipping him back from the temporary hospital later tomorrow.

His mother had broken in, still crying, "He could be home as early as next week."

Xtina had soothed her as much as she could.

Xtina glanced over at Jacob, who sat in the corner, his face a little pale. She knew it was probably because his family was there. She knew he wanted answers, but he also knew they wouldn't all come that night.

After his parents had gone back to Mike's house for the night, Jacob stood up and walked over to the fireplace, holding out his hands for warmth.

"Okay," he said, turning back to the room. Xtina sat next to Mike while Jessie was in her mother's old rocking chair, looking a little lost. "Tell me what the hell is happening to me? Why I'm seeing…" He motioned, taking a deep breath. "Things."

"I wish I knew," Mike said, turning slightly to her. "Any ideas?"

She nodded, then stood up slowly. "Yes, but we're not all here, yet…" Just then her doorbell chimed and she took a deep breath. "That will be her."

"Her?" Jessie asked. "Who, her?"

Xtina turned to the room and smiled. "A piece

to our puzzle."

She held her breath as she walked towards the door. She wasn't too sure what she'd find on the other side. All she knew was that more power was coming soon. As soon as Ethan made it home.

When she opened the door, she looked into the most beautiful crystal blue eyes she'd ever seen. Peace settled in her mind and heart, then power filled the entire room.

Other books by Jill Sanders

The Pride Series
Finding Pride
Discovering Pride
Returning Pride
Lasting Pride
Serving Pride
Red Hot Christmas
My Sweet Valentine
Return To Me
Rescue Me

The Secret Series
Secret Seduction
Secret Pleasure
Secret Guardian
Secret Passions
Secret Identity
Secret Sauce

The West Series
Loving Lauren
Taming Alex
Holding Haley
Missy's Moment
Breaking Travis
Roping Ryan
Wild Bride
Corey's Catch

The Grayton Series
Last Resort
Someday Beach
Rip Current
In Too Deep
Swept Away

Lucky Series
Unlucky In Love
Sweet Resolve

Silver Cove Series
Silver Lining
French Kiss

Coming this fall...
Entangled – *A Paranormal Romance Series*
The Awakening
The Beckoning... Spring 2017
The Ascension... Summer/Fall 2017

For a complete list of books, visit JillSanders.com

This is a work of fiction. Names, characters, places, and incidents are either the product of the author's imagination or are used fictitiously, and any resemblance to actual persons, living or dead, business establishments, events, or locales is entirely coincidental.

THE AWAKENING
PRINT ISBN: 978-1-942896-75-3
DIGITAL ISBN: 978-1-942896-73-9
Copyright © 2016 Jill Sanders
Copyeditor: Erica Ellis – inkdeepediting.com

About the Author

 Jill Sanders is *The New York Times* and *USA Today* bestselling author of the Pride Series, Secret Series, West Series, Grayton Series, Lucky Series, and Silver Cove romance novels. She continues to lure new readers with her sweet and sexy stories. Her books are available in every English-speaking country and in audiobooks as well as being translated into different languages.

Born as an identical twin to a large family, she was raised in the Pacific Northwest and later relocated to Colorado for college and a successful IT career before discovering her talent as a writer. She now makes her home along the Emerald Coast in Florida where she enjoys the beach, hiking, swimming, wine tasting, and of course writing.

Connect with Jill on Facebook:
http://fb.com/JillSandersBooks

Twitter: @JillMSanders or visit her Web site at http://JillSanders.com

Made in the USA
Middletown, DE
25 September 2020